Ken Rodgers

The
Gods of Angkor Wat

Short Stories

BK Publications
Eagle, Idaho

First electronic edition published November 2012
First print edition July 2014
Copyright © 2004, 2005, 2006, 2007, 2008, 2009, 2010, 2011,
2012, 2013, 2014 by Ken Rodgers

ISBN: 0-9794521-6-3

Published in the United States by BK Publications, Eagle, Idaho.

All of the characters in these short stories are fictitious, and any
resemblance to persons living or dead is purely coincidental.

To schedule a reading or interview contact Ken Rodgers via
kennethrodgers.com.

Several stories in this volume appeared in somewhat
different form in the following publications:

"The Gods of Angkor Wat" in *VerbSap*, 2006

"Big Thunder" in *Ascent Aspirations*, 2007

"Routine" in *34th Parallel*, 2007, and the anthology
Ashes Caught on the Edge of Light, Winterhawk Press

"Brown Sparrows" in *The Farallon Review*, 2008

"Party" in *Fiction Attic*, 2005

"Heezey's Wake," in RomanCandles.com, 2004

"Pugilist" in *The Farallon Review*, 2010

This book is for
Ray Fred Kelly and Uncle Robbie

Big THANK YOUs are in order to Jamey Genna and Guy Biederman for their most valuable assistance with these stories.

Much thanks, too, to Jeri Dobrowski of Lamesteer Publishing & Graphics.

And as always, a big HOORAH to my editor and main muse, Betty Rodgers.

Ken has a fine eye and an excellent ear and a huge and courageous heart. Whatever his subject, his writing is always unflinchingly honest, and I've grown to depend on the way that honesty both scathes and celebrates the subjects he writes about.
— Jean Hegland
   Author of *Into the Forest* and *Windfalls*

Contents

Kaw-Liga

The cottonwood tree dropped too many dry, yellow leaves that took forever to rake. When I built piles the breeze invaded and scattered them, forcing me to rake again and again.

It took all day but I crammed the dead leaves into the big cardboard box which I dragged to the alley and emptied a bunch of times so the garbage men could pick up the big pile. Our dog Ace made it hard because he kept prancing and frolicking through the piles, dropping his ugly old baseball in the leaves. He wanted to play fetch. I didn't have time because when Daddy got home I wanted to be done, so after a while I had to kick at him every time he came around. That's how you train dogs, make them mind. Or you can hit them with a rake.

Ace is Sissybug's dog—he's supposed to be mine, but he's really hers.

When Daddy came home he got out of his red Texaco pickup in his army-green Texaco uniform with the name patch over his right front pocket that said, "Jimmy Joe." He put his hands on his hips and said, "Hey, good buddy, what you been doing?"

I smiled.

He walked over and ran his big, tanned hand through my fine, white hair and said, "Looks pretty good, good buddy."

Then he dug in his army-green Texaco pants and handed

me a shiny quarter.

He looked at Ace sitting with his butt against the screen door at the front of our house. Daddy whistled and snapped his fingers. Ace stood up and shook his butt and stood on three legs and then a different three legs and grinned his dog grin. But he didn't come to us.

Daddy glanced at me and said, "What's wrong with Ace?"

I looked at the ground and shrugged.

Daddy grabbed my shoulder. "You ain't been beating him, have you?"

His big fingers bit my flesh. "Ow, Daddy. That hurts."

He squeezed harder.

I cried, "No, Daddy. I didn't hit him."

He said, "If I find you've been beating that dog, I'll take that quarter away and show you how a beating feels, boy."

I threw my arms around his big right leg and sobbed, "I love Ace."

Daddy let go of my shoulder and rubbed my hair again. "Okay, good buddy."

After we went into the house I told Momma, "I want to go to Jackson's and buy something," and she asked me what and I said, "I don't know, just something."

She didn't say "no" so I ran out the back door of the house and across the concrete floor of the back porch and slammed the screen door. I sprinted across the browning grass in the yard and through the wire gate into the alley. I clutched that quarter in my right hand. I felt the ridges on the edges, felt the head of that man on the quarter pressed into my palm. I heard Ace coming and then the voice of Sissybug, "Wayne, wait."

Waiting for Ace was sort of okay, because he's supposed to be my pet, but not for Sissybug. She's my sister. I don't like her. She's twelve.

I didn't stop. She yelled, "Daddy gave me my own quarter." When she said that my insides felt like they fell through my feet.

The backyards on both sides of the dirt alley were lined with oleanders and the dust made them look tan instead of green. A lot of dogs barked as we hurried past.

I picked up a rock and threw it at a white pit bull that lived behind a sheepherder's page-wire fence. "Stop barking at my dog. I love him."

Sissybug grinned and said, "If you love him, how come you hit him all the time?"

I stuck my tongue out at her and ran to Jackson's store. Ace stayed with Sissybug.

I shuffled in the back door of Jackson's, kicking the toes of my tennis shoes into the wood floor, and went straight to the bubble gum jar. Sissybug hurried in behind. She jabbered at Mrs. Jackson, "How much stuff can we get for fifty cents?"

I glared at her. I ain't sharing, I thought.

I heard Ace's claws scratching the floorboards as he stayed close to Sissybug. Nobody can touch Sissybug except me and Daddy and Momma and Granny. Ace bites anybody else that even gets close to her.

Ace bit the milkman and he bit the mailman, too. Daddy says if he bites anybody else he's "going to shoot the worthless son-of-a-bitch."

Momma says, "I can't understand how that dog got so mean."

Daddy says, "What do you expect? He's a damned dog."

Momma says, "We haven't had him that long. He wasn't like that when he was a pup."

I remember when we got Ace. A big, long sheepherder truck pulled up in the dirt road in front of our house. The silver trailer with all the holes in the side was full of sheep. I could smell them from inside the house—the scent of moldy cottonwood leaves and dirt and the way the desert smells after rain.

When the truck drove up and honked the big horn on top, Momma smiled and said, "Honey, go outside and see what it is."

She stood and held the front door open for me as I walked out. I stopped on the sidewalk outside as a tall, thin man wearing a big straw cowboy hat got out of the maroon-colored cab. He carried a black and white puppy.

When he stepped to the ground he said, "Come and get him."

I looked back at Momma and shrugged. She laughed and said, "Go get him. He's yours."

At the grocery store I heard Mr. Jackson talking to Ace real soft and easy. He had put his cigarette out because Sissybug gets asthma from cigarette smoke. She gets asthma from everything. I think she fakes it.

Mrs. Jackson leaned against the checkout counter talking to Sissybug. They talked about a lime-green coffee mug and a Big Hunk and an Almond Joy that sat on the counter. The screen door on the front entrance slammed and somebody came in. I was looking at the boxes of Milk Duds and Jujubees, so I didn't see who it was but I heard Ace run up and a scaredy-cat got ahold of my neck because Ace was going to bite somebody but he didn't, and I heard someone say, "Hey, Ace, how you doing, boy?"

Something wasn't right because I recognized the voice belonged to the Okie who lived right across the dirt road from us. Elmore Dixon. Ace's supposed to bite him 'cause we don't like him or his kind. Ever since Korea he sits on the front porch at night with his guitar and sings Hank Williams songs until after midnight. Daddy says it's because of Korea.

Momma says, "He can't sing."

Daddy says, "Son-of-a-bitch keeps me awake."

Daddy gets up before the sun to go to work. Daddy says, "He butchers them Hank Williams songs."

Momma says, "You can't butcher something as bad as Hank Williams songs." She likes Bing Crosby. Daddy's favorite song is "Kaw-Liga"—a song about a wooden Indian.

I think it's silly. Whoever heard of a wooden Indian? We got lots of Indians come to our town on Saturday morning to get drunk on skid row and ain't none of them wooden.

But Ace didn't bite Okie Elmore. When I walked around the candy rack and looked at Okie Elmore he was kneeling down running his hands through Ace's black and white fur, whispering something in his ear. Sissybug was standing on one leg smiling at the two of them. Ace sniffed Okie Elmore's leg and the silver tips of his old cowboy boots.

I hissed, "Ace, get over here."

Elmore looked at me with a sad face. His brown eyes looked like they were going to start leaking tears. He always looked like that. Ace slunk over to me with his tail between his legs.

Sissybug said, "Wayne. Mind your manners."

I said, "He's my dog," even though he really wasn't.

Ace walked around in a tight circle at my feet. His pink tongue stuck out the side of his mouth. When he looked at me it was like he wanted to smile.

Sissybug said, "I'm going to tell Momma that somebody needs to teach you some manners."

Okie Elmore smiled and waved his hands like nothing mattered. "Don't worry about it."

His voice had an Okie drawl. Momma talks bad about people with Okie drawls. She says stuff like, "Just shows ignorance. Lack of education."

Sissybug inched real close to Elmore and looked up at him. She stood on her right leg, her left penny loafer on top of the right one. She twisted a little bit, left then right.

I said, "Momma's going to get mad."

Sissybug smiled at Okie Elmore and shrugged. When she looked at me she pinched her face into the ugliest smooch look you ever saw and stuck her tongue out at me.

She said, "We need to go. Momma's got dinner on."

I said, "I haven't got my stuff."

She said, "I got what Momma told me to get."

I said, "But Daddy gave me my quarter. I don't want all this old junk."

Sissybug raised her eyebrows at the Jacksons as if she didn't know me and said, "Momma won't let you have what she doesn't want you to have."

I knew the truth of that so I walked to the counter and looked at the loot lying there ... a bunch of bubble gum in bright red and yellow wrappers, an Almond Joy (obviously for Sissybug), a Big Hunk (they're okay), and a Hershey bar with almonds (I like those). Mrs. Jackson piled the packages of gum into the coffee mug. I pointed at the mug and announced, "I ain't paying for that."

Sissybug kicked my shins. "Shush. It's for Daddy. Don't you ever think of anybody but yourself?"

I handed over my quarter.

I went out the back screen door and heard Sissybug still yapping at the Jacksons. I said to Ace, "Get over here."

He sat on his haunches and put his head down with his tongue out the side of his mouth again like he was trying to smile.

"Come on. Get over here."

He walked my direction a step or two then stopped again. I knelt down and whistled and snapped my fingers and said, "Oh, Ace boy. Come on, boy."

He came with his haunches down, tail jammed up between his hind legs against his stomach, his tongue out, panting. When he got close I reached over and yanked ahold of his collar and shook it. Then I whacked him on the head. The hard bone above his eyes hurt my hand. He pulled away and let out a yip and as I stood I kicked him hard in the side. "How come you didn't bite the Okie?"

He jerked away, slinked over and sat by the back door. I stood up straight and slapped my right leg. "I said, get over here."

But he sat there on his haunches, breathing like he'd just run down the alley from one end to the other, swiveling his head back and forth, his eyes looking at me like he didn't love me. I walked to get him but Sissybug came out the screen door with a brown paper bag and said, "Let's go." She was wheezing like an asthma attack was coming on. I wondered what got her so excited.

Ace stood up and got Sissybug between him and me. I sneered at her. "What were you doing in there?"

"None of your business."

I said, "I'm telling about him."

She laughed. "You do and I'll tell about the peaches you stole from Mr. Green."

I didn't say anything more about it as we walked back to eat dinner. Ace shot down the alley over a ditch and into a vacant lot. He chased a chuckwalla lizard into its hole under a mesquite tree. There were lots of scrawny mesquite trees in that lot, and greasewood, too, and an old car with no wheels that me and the neighborhood kids beat up pretty good with a rusty old piston and a pinch bar.

I said, "Let me carry the cup."

Sissybug ignored me.

I said, "I want to give it to him."

She smirked and said, "Not yet, stupid. It's not Daddy's birthday yet."

I said, "Well, when is it?"

"It's coming."

"When?"

Ace came back with the lizard's tail hanging out of his mouth.

Sissybug said, "He got her."

I said, "No he didn't. Their tails break off when something gets them."

She said, "Uhn-uh."

"Is too so. Mrs. Carver said."

"First grade doesn't know."

"Knows as much as sixth."

"Well, you can't carry it."

"What?"

"This stuff."

I kicked a rusty tin can out of the alley.

I said, "Okay, Permelia Hattie."

"Don't you call me that."

"That's your name."

"Uhn-uh, name's Sissybug. That's what Daddy calls me."

Sissybug's real name is Permelia. That's Granny's name. Sissybug got laughed at at school so my daddy calls her Sissybug. Sissybug's middle name is after Granny's older sister, Aunt Hattie. She smokes a corncob pipe. Daddy says, "Meaner than a Christ-Almighty Marine DI." Aunt Hattie's corncob pipe smoke gives Sissybug asthma.

"Permelia."

"I'm telling Daddy."

"Tattle-tale."

Ace peed on an oleander bush just inside the gate of our yard.

Sissybug said, "Ace. Stop that."

I laughed. "Daddy says that's what dogs do. Marking spots."

"What kind of spots?"

"Dog spots."

"What for?"

I said, "Only dogs know."

"You don't know anything. It's territorial and sexual."

"You don't know anything either."

She shot back, "Do too."

I said, "What's sexual?" I said, "I'm telling Daddy."

She stopped. "Telling him what?"

"About you and Elmore."

She looked past me. Her eyes looked like buttons on Momma's brown coat. She hissed, "Isn't anything to tell." The setting sunlight lit up the little specks of spit that followed each of her words.

"Is too."

"No there isn't."

I said, "Let me give him the cup."

She made her mouth like Granny does when she's going to switch me. Then she shoved the bag at me and turned so fast I almost dropped it.

As she opened the door into the back porch she stuck out her tongue. When she did, she curled it up like the leaves I'd raked earlier that day, except it wasn't dry. It was wet.

She flipped her curly hair-do at me and turned and pranced into the house. Ace tried to follow her but as I went inside I caught him between the screen door and the jamb. He stopped wagging his tail and stared up at me with big, sad eyes. I kicked him in the side and pulled the door into his ribs with my one free hand as hard as I could and hissed, "You're on her side. You got to stay outside."

He let his head hang as I used my legs to push him back out into the yard.

After dinner Momma let me chew a piece of bubble gum because I ate my spinach. She thinks she has to give me things so I'll eat spinach. She doesn't have to because I know I'll get muscles like Popeye if I eat my greens, but I don't tell her that. I like the bubble gum.

Thunder came through as me and Daddy listened to a football game on the radio. ASC was "beating hell" out of some other team when the lights went out and the radio, too. Daddy likes to say "beating hell" and lots of other things I'm not supposed to say or I get my mouth washed out with Ivory soap.

The rain came in and it was going sideways and the wind screamed like children all around the corners of the house. Big lightning ran through town and bombed us with loud thunder. I thought about hiding under the bed but Daddy gets mad when I do that. He says, "Stop acting like a girl." Besides, Popeye wouldn't hide; he'd make big biceps and fix it.

Momma made me and Sissybug go to bed but I was so scared of the thunder I got into bed with Sissybug and shivered. She said, "Now, good buddy, nothing to be afraid of." She put her arms around me.

I dozed for I don't know how long and then awoke in a full sweat next to Sissybug. I tried to move but she held me tight. Out in the black night I heard Okie Elmore singing on his front porch, "Kaw-Liga was a wood-head Indian, leaning by the door."

I said, "Here he goes. A lot of howling worse than Ace does."

Sissybug whispered in my ear, "I like it."

She was behind me and had her arms tight around my stomach. She reached up and rubbed the nipple of my right titty.

I squirmed and said, "Stop."

She said, "Hush up."

The thunder boomed off to the west.

Elmore went on, "He fell in love with an Indian maiden over by the antique store."

She said, "This is how you make love."

My nipples felt hard. I said, "What's that, making love?"

Outside, the peepers sang their irrigation ditch songs.

She whispered, "Don't talk so loud." Then she said, "It's sexual. Roll over."

I did and noticed something was wrong with my pee-pee. Sissybug grabbed both my hands and put them up under her t-shirt. I felt her titties. They were little and soft and I could squeeze them.

She giggled and said, "Not so hard."

Her nipples were hard.

Elmore sang, "Poor old Kaw-Liga, never had a kiss."

There was a long-tailed chuckwalla lizard inside my tummy. I could feel its tail flicking and when Sissybug grabbed my hand and stuck it between her legs and I felt a little patch of hair I started to wonder how she got hair down there but the thought really didn't stick because that lizard suddenly began racing around like Ace was after it, up and down from my stomach to my throat. Up and down.

Sissy was wet and I whispered, "Did you pee?"

When she answered her voice was husky and didn't sound like Sissybug, "No, that's my sexual."

I wondered what that meant as the lizard went into both my legs at the same time and Elmore sang, "Well he stood there as lonely as could be 'cause his heart's an ol' oak knotty tree."

And then Sissybug was on her back and put her arms around my back and pulled me on top of her body and then reached down and got my pee-pee in her hand and I wanted to giggle because my pee-pee was as hard as old Kaw-Liga's head and she whispered, "We're going to make love," and I thought my heart would slam right through my skin and the bedroom door flew open and Daddy had me in his big, brown hand. He had me by the skin over my ribs and I could feel every inch of his thumb and fingers as they bit into me.

I screamed, "No, Daddy."

He jerked me around and carried me like a bag of dog chow and held me away as I dangled and kicked my legs. He undid his belt buckle with his left hand and pulled the belt out of the loops. I heard its tail slap as it came off. I yelled, "No, Daddy. I'm Good Buddy."

He didn't say nothing. The belt bit into my legs, my back. I screamed but could still hear Okie Elmore singing. "Kaw-Ligaaaaaaaaaaaaaaa, Oh-u-oh."

Then Daddy yelled, "You're not my good buddy. No buddy of mine. You're not mine."

And more Elmore, "And she could never respond yes or no."

When Daddy wore himself out he threw me on the couch and over my sobs and Elmore's wailing I could hear Momma slapping Sissybug's mouth as she said, over and over, "Where'd you learn that trash? Where'd you learn that, Permelia?"

Sissybug was talking but she was crying and wheezing so much I couldn't catch a word. Besides, my sobs were hurting me too hard. I knew she'd get out of trouble because of asthma.

Once I heard Daddy say, "I ought to get my shotgun."

The next morning, Sunday, we didn't go to church. Daddy hauled Sissybug off to live with Aunt Hattie. Sissybug didn't like that. She hates the smell of that corncob pipe. She kept grabbing her chest and wheezing the whole morning and when she got in Daddy's Texaco pickup, too. I was real glad we got out of going to church. Besides, the welts still burned real bad and the skin over my ribs where he grabbed me looked like a black-and-blue handprint.

Next day before I went to school, I told Ace to come to me, but he must have sensed Sissybug was gone away to Aunt Hattie's so he just sat by the back door. When he didn't do what I said I put my arms around his neck and hugged him tight but he acted like he didn't know me.

I yelled at him, "Ace, you're my dog."

He turned his muzzle up and rolled his big eyes at me, then looked away.

I said, "You're my dog, too."

But he just ran his tongue along his teeth and black gums and looked into the neighbor's yard.

I said, "Okay for you."

I got the grass rake and started beating Ace with it. Momma came out and took the rake away from me and hit me with it on the back and legs and made the welts and bruises Daddy gave me burn all over again.

Momma said that after I went to school Ace bit the mailman. Daddy came home from Aunt Hattie's and got his shotgun and tied Ace in the back of his red Texaco pickup. He came home after dark but he didn't bring Ace with him.

Daddy doesn't call me Good Buddy now. He doesn't call

me anything. He just sits in his chair in the living room and listens to his big oak-paneled radio.

Momma don't talk much either. She did tell me that maybe next month we'll go see Sissybug. That's good because I got something to tell her. Okie Elmore's gone. He moved somewhere and won't be singing that awful "Kaw-Liga" no more.

The Gods of Angkor Wat

Mrs. A brought in a slide show of some place called Angkor Wat. There were weird buildings with towers like stacks of hard ice cream you can't get at the Dairy Queen. She called them pagodas. She went there in the summer. Before I got in third grade. As she talked, she paraded around the front of the class with her red hair and freckles. Her hair stood out against the dark wood paneling of our classroom. She went there with her husband and daughter, to Angkor Wat, in some French place in Asia. Mrs. A's daughter, Chrissy, has red hair, too, and she wears it short. Chrissy can run fast and punch hard. She's in fourth grade. When she gets promoted next year, she'll go to North School. Then she won't hit me all the time.

While Mrs. A was showing the pictures on the screen, me and Elver were shooting spitballs at each other. He told me he was going to whip my ass at lunchtime. Sometimes he's my best friend. We go to church together where his dad's a deacon. His dad's a sheriff's deputy, too. Last summer Elver's dad whipped me with a willow switch. I taught Elver how to say "Fuck." We stood out in the yard in the irrigation ditch and yelled, "Fuck, fuck, fuck."

Elver's mother called his dad. He came home in his sheriff's car. It has a neat siren on it which was whining when he arrived. After he got out of the car, he stripped a willow switch and got after me and Elver. After a little while he sent Elver in the house and said to me, "Boy, I'm going to whip that vulgarity out of your mouth."

I hopped around as he whipped me. I could feel it through my jeans. It hurt, but not as much as when my father whips me. Father gets me barelegged and raises ugly welts. I didn't tell Elver's dad his whipping wasn't near as bad as my father's. I screamed and cried a lot so's he'd stop before it did start to hurt too much.

Elver wanted to kick my ass today because I hit his cousin Nick in the head this morning at recess. We had been playing Red Rover. Some girls were playing, too. Jinny, mostly. She lets me kiss her. I started last year. Kissing her. This morning she let Nick kiss her, too. He was holding hands with Jinny when I called, "Red Rover, Red Rover, let Nicky come over."

He was laughing as he ran towards us. Like he was going to break right through our line. He came straight at me. I could see a shiny spot above his right eyebrow. He was smiling. I don't know why I did it. Hit him, I mean. I just hit him right on that shiny spot. He fell on the ground and kicked his legs around. He screamed. The kids got in a circle around him and clucked like quail in a mesquite thicket. I was standing alone. I looked at my fist. The knuckles throbbed. I liked that feeling.

I had to go see Mrs. A. She's the principal, too. She made me sit outside the office for a long time. The secretary wouldn't look at me. I stared at the big calendar behind her. It showed a painting of Santa Claus trying to get down a chimney.

Mrs. A came out of her office and frowned at me. Her face was so red it was hard to see her freckles. She made me march in and stand in front of her desk. She walked around with a paddle in her hand. She walked behind me. I covered my butt with my hands. She slapped the paddle on her leg.

She said, "Ennis, why did you hit Nick?"

I looked at the hardwood floor. There was a lot of dirt in

the joints where the flooring pieces came together.

She said, "Ennis, why did you hit Nick?"

I said, "I don't know."

She said, "Ennis, you are always hitting somebody. Why?"

I didn't answer. I stood there looking at the floor. I stood there with my hands over my butt. She didn't whip me.

After Mrs. A stopped talking about Angkor Wat, it was time for lunch. We had grilled cheese sandwiches and tomato soup. I don't like cheese and I don't like tomatoes. I threw my lunch in the garbage can along with my empty milk carton. I ate the bread pudding.

Outside I saw some older kids playing by the picnic tables. I went over there. Mrs. A's daughter was one of them. She had a magnifying glass. She was burning something into the top of the table. I walked over and watched the way the sun came through the lens and pinched down to a tiny, white-hot dot that made the wood in the table top smoke. She was writing, "Chrissy loves," but there wasn't any name there yet, I mean the name of who she loved. I got up close. She looked up at me and frowned, then stuck her tongue out.

Right then somebody pushed me from behind. It was Elver. I turned around and he threw a punch at me. But he missed. I got him in a headlock and Dutch-rubbed him. I could feel his hair underneath my knuckles. He squirmed. I kicked his feet out from under him. I fell on top. I whispered in his ear, "Fucker, fucker, fucker."

He threw me over and started to hit me in the face. He knocked my glasses off. Tears got in my eye. Chrissy A was screaming, "Hit him, Elver. Kick his ass."

I got ahold of his hair and pulled hard. He stopped hitting me and whined. I yanked harder and he tried to get away.

Someone yelled, "Cheater."

I got behind him and bit him on the side of the neck just

below his left ear. He jerked hard, but I sank my teeth in deeper. There was blood in my mouth. I liked the taste of it, the way it reminded me of tinfoil.

Somebody grabbed me and threw me to the ground. Through the tears in my eyes I could see it was Chrissy. She was hissing under her breath. I couldn't make the words out, but I didn't like the sound.

The playground proctor, Mrs. C, came along and grabbed me by the back of my shirt and hauled me off to see Mrs. A. This time Mrs. A wasn't so nice. She'd had holes drilled in the paddle. I could hear the air sluice through them as she swung it. I got five swats. They burned like my father's belt. Mrs. A was little. Her whipping surprised me. I didn't let her know, though. My guts hurt from the fact that I refused to cry. She called my momma at work. Momma's boss gets mad when people call her at work. My momma wasn't there, though. I was glad. Momma would tell Father. He'd whip me, too, most likely.

After she swatted me, Mrs. A said, "Why did you bite him?"

I looked at the ground. She shook me by the shoulders, "Why did you bite him?"

"He was whipping me."

She rolled her eyes at Mrs. C, who was standing there watching.

Back in the class, Mrs. A talked about adding numbers. I kept looking at Elver. One of his eyes was swelling up and turning black. I felt like my chest would explode. I liked that feeling.

At recess, Mrs. C came and got me off the playground and took me to Mrs. A's office, again. I put my hands over my butt as we walked. Mrs. A said, "Ennis, your grandfather has passed away."

I stared at her. I still held my hands over my butt. I thought, must be my father's father. The other one's dead.

She said, "Ennis, your grandfather has passed away. Do

you understand me, honey?"

I nodded. I didn't know my grandfather. Just his black-and-white milk cows, and the old horse out in the barn-yard. And his three-legged dog. The yellow one with the concrete block tied around a chain that was looped around his neck. I didn't know my grandfather.

Mrs. A said, "Honey, after school you go right to your momma's office. She wants you to walk right over there. She'll wait there so she can take you to a babysitter while your daddy and she go to see about your grandfather. Understand, honey?"

I nodded.

After recess, Mrs. A talked about spelling words. Every time she said another word, I'd look away from her red hair and the dark paneling. I'd look outside at the Chinese elm trees. Their naked branches reminded me of the termite tubes that ran along the walls of the barn where my grandfather kept his black-and-white milk cows.

Once, when I was looking out the window at the old stone church across the street, I heard Mrs. A clear her throat. I looked at her real fast so's she wouldn't think I wasn't listening to her. She was staring at me. I looked at the floor.

After school, I walked out the front gate and headed for Momma's office. On the sidewalk in front of the school, Chrissy A and Thel, Elver's other cousin, were leaning against the chain-link fence. I tried to get by, but when Chrissy hissed at me I said, "Fuck you."

Thel jumped at me and I hit him in the nose. I felt it cave in. Blood shot out and ran down the front of his shirt. He looked at me like one of those Saturday Matinee movie cowboy bad guys looks when the hero shoots him. He was crying. The sight of him crying made my insides feel like they were boiling over. My face got hot. I kicked him in the nuts. He screamed and fell to his knees. Chrissy grabbed me and started slapping me on the face. She knocked my glasses off. I hit her in the breasts. That's where I hit my older sister when she messes with me. When I hit my sister there, she folds her arms over them and runs away. When I hit Chrissy, she stopped slapping me and yelled, "Don't hit me there, it causes cancer."

Those words were like worms digging on the inside of my ears. I punched her in the breasts as hard as I could, once, then again and again. I could hear other students rooting. Chrissy tried to get away from me. I tripped her. She whopped when she hit the concrete. I pulled her over on her back and punched some more and every time my fists hit those breasts I hissed at her, "Die, fucker, die."

Mrs. C suddenly had me by the arm and yanked me around and started kicking me in the butt, saying, "Don't you ever hit a girl. Don't you ever hit a girl. Especially not there."

Her breath was hot on the side of my face as she said those words. I thought I could smell onions. Her face was as white as the spots on my grandfather's black-and-white cows.

Jinny was standing behind the crowd looking at me. I couldn't read her face. Nick was there with a knot over his right eyebrow. He was smiling.

Mrs. A was real mad, too. She said, "Ennis, I've seen you in here too many times."

She grabbed her paddle. "Ennis, do you understand?'

I looked at her. She was lit up like one of those red Christmas tree lights hanging on the tree in our living room.

"Ennis, do you understand?"

By now, Momma would be swearing under her breath. Father always fumed when we were late. I suddenly thought about those pictures Mrs. A showed of Angkor Wat. I could see the pagodas sticking up. Mrs. A said that they worshiped other gods at Angkor Wat. I wondered what Elver's dad would think about those other gods. He was always looking at heaven and talking real loud about our god. I wondered if my grandfather had gone to see our god, if he was talking to him about milk cows.

"Ennis, do you understand?"

Momma would be here soon. To see why I was late. Father would be here, too. He hates to be late.

I covered my butt with my hands, noticed the dirty joints in the floor. I heard the hiss of the paddle. It reminded me of the sound of milk hitting a tin pail when my grandfather squeezed the tits of one of his black-and-white cows.

China-Burma-India

The white-wings landed in the road and Daddy said, "They're gravelling."

He slowed the truck and grabbed his shotgun and nodded at me to get mine.

He said, "We'll Arkansas them.'

"Arkansas?"

He grimaced. "Shoot them on the ground."

"Is that sporting?"

He snorted, "No."

I didn't say anything, just looked at the white-winged doves pecking at the pea gravel.

CG Mountain waited at the end of the road. A eucalyptus tree that must have been over a hundred feet tall stood there. Behind the tree, you could see rows of saguaro cactus growing up the side of the ridges. They reminded me of rows of French soldiers I had seen attacking the Germans in that World War I movie with Kirk Douglas. The cacti blended in with the gray and black granite.

"Pay attention now, Son. When I stop, get out and shoot the birds."

I asked, "What if they fly?"

He frowned and shook his head. "Shoot them."

He eased in the clutch and stepped on the brakes and the shoes squeaked. The fifteen or so dove sitting in the road looked up and tensed like they wanted to fly.

He said, "Steady now. Get out and kill as many as you

can, Son."

I pushed down on the door handle and it croaked when it opened. I slipped off the seat and landed on the ground. My lower jaw snapped against my upper teeth when I hit the dirt road.

Daddy stood outside with his double-barrel at his shoulder. He whispered, "Come on now, Son, they're going to fly if we don't shoot."

I stepped clear of the open pickup door and threw my shotgun to my shoulder. The barrel felt like it was too long. I thought I'd fall down from its weight. I heard Daddy snort. I pointed the gun at the place where the dove worked at the gravel and let fly just before Daddy did. Four dove scrabbled in circles in the dirt. Another one lay on its back and flapped its wings. I heard the slap, slap, slap.

In the meantime, Daddy chambered two more shells and dropped two more white-wings before they got too far. He trotted out among the jumping cactus and greasewood to find them before they ran off and shimmied down a rat hole.

I knew what my job was. I did it a lot of times before Daddy bought me my gun. I was the bird dog.

I slung the shotgun muzzle down over my right forearm and marched to where the five dove lay in the road. One tried to run off, but I chased it down and stomped on it and I heard it squeak as I laid my gun on the ground and reached down and picked the dove up. I felt its heart pound. It struggled and flapped its wings as I held it away from my body. I knew my job. I closed my eyes and yanked its head off. Hot blood shot across my fingers.

Two others birds made attempts to get away, but I beheaded them too and then picked up the two really dead ones and just for fun, pulled their heads off and stuffed the bodies in the pocket of my too-big bird vest.

When I looked up, Daddy stood smiling at me like I was something he was proud he made, like a bookcase or an end table, but that wasn't possible, he couldn't make anything. He took his hammer or screwdriver and smashed and gouged when things didn't go the way he thought they ought to. Momma says that's what he does, too.

He pointed up the road. "Let's go up to the well beneath that tree and clean these birds."

I knew what that meant. It was another part of my job.

We climbed into the truck and drove off.

I saw birds fly in and out of the tall tree Daddy was going to.

Fields of grain grew on both sides of the road. I said, "Daddy, what is that grain?" Irrigation wells sat in the corners of each field. I liked how their black smoke stacks jutted into the sky and as the engines throbbed, the covers of the stacks jumped up and down.

"Milo maize, Son."

Then we drove past cotton fields with white tufts busting out of the cotton squares. Wells thrummed in those fields, too.

I said, "Daddy, is that cotton ready to pick?"

Irrigation hoses lined the ditches, watering the cotton.

"I guess, Son."

"Why they still irrigating?"

"I don't know, Son. Maybe they want to get some more cotton to mature."

I didn't believe he didn't know.

I said, "How come the dove eat gravel?"

He smiled, "I'll show you."

As we got closer it seemed like the tall tree up there was full of birds, a whole universe of birds.

"Are those dove, Daddy?"

"I don't know, Son. Maybe."

"Can we kill them?"

"If they don't all leave."

I slipped the bolt back on my gun to see if there was a round in the chamber.

He barked. "Be careful. Don't shoot me, or worse, blow your foot off."

I nodded.

The engine on the truck thudded at a slow pace as we crept up the road. It seemed like we'd never get there. I rubbed my shotgun's stock with both hands. We passed a patch of ground with another well that shot water into a ditch.

Two saguaro cacti grew close by. One had both arms up like a Nazi surrendering in one of the Audie Murphy war movies we watched all the time. The other looked like it held up one arm to tell us to stop. That reminded me of Daddy's forearms and his tattoos. That saguaro's other arm pointed down like it wanted to draw its pistol and shoot us. Brett Maverick or Johnny Ringo.

Daddy drove right beneath the tall eucalyptus tree. Dove flew in and out like they didn't know we existed. The bark on the tree hung like skin that my pet lizard shed when he was still alive.

Daddy killed the truck's engine and we sat there. I wiped sweat out of my eyes.

I looked at Daddy and the side of his prominent nose with blackheads that looked like dots. His eyes narrowed and he had his tongue sticking out the side of his mouth.

I said, "Can we kill some, Daddy?"

He looked into the rearview mirror at the setting sun. "We got about five minutes, Son. Then we won't be legal."

I jumped out and sneaked around the back of the truck so the sun wasn't in my eyes.

I glanced at Daddy as he stepped out. He leaned through the window of the open driver's-side door. He looked weird as he stood on his right leg, his left boot on top of his right. A Salem hung from his lips. He mumbled, "Go on now, Son. Kill some."

I looked at all the long leaves of the tree. Their shape reminded me of the curved bronze scimitar that sat on

Daddy's nightstand. That one he brought home from India after the war.

I spotted a fat white-wing on a branch. I wondered if it was too far to shoot. I didn't want to miss with Daddy watching. The bird swiveled its gray head around, left, then right. I saw its right eye rolling around like a large BB. I heard Daddy chuckle. I looked up. He pulled the Salem from his lips and smiled at me as smoke got in his eyes. He nodded and said, "Go on, Son."

I sighted in and squeezed the trigger as I shut my eyes and the gun kicked my shoulder and the bang swirled around my head and when I opened my eyes the branch was empty and then I heard a plop.

My heart thumped and I searched the ground and there it was, like a gray rock. A few feathers floated above with some gnats.

I searched the tree to see if there were any more dove. I reached down and picked the bird up. Daddy said, "Let's go now, Son. You scared the rest of them off and they won't be back until it gets too dark for us to hunt. Let's get these birds cleaned."

I nodded. He grabbed a plastic bowl and some poultry scissors from under the truck seat and walked over to the tank where the well water roared out of the ground. The sound of the pump engine swirled around the inside of the concrete tank. Daddy set his tools down and yelled, "Get the birds and put them on that concrete edge." He pointed to the lip of the tank.

Two pumps sat close together. I didn't like the sound of their hammering. They clanged like a thousand steel hammers banging a thousand times a second. I glanced at their dark rusty engines which reminded me of the engine inside Daddy's truck. The engine on the left side of the tank shook on its concrete pad.

I took the bird bag and set it on the ground. Black ants made a trail through some Johnson grass. Pipes from both pumps emptied into the square concrete tank. Water shot from the pipes and around the tank and then into a cement ditch that ran alongside the road.

Daddy's arms stretched out. I stared again, for the millionth time, at his tattoos. One was of a woman with a veil across her face. It was tinted pink and blue. That was on top of his left forearm and every time my mother looked at it she'd look away. Sometimes her jaws got tight.

The tattoo on his right arm was a chevron emblem shaped like a shield with a sun and a star and faded red and flesh-tinted stripes running up and down and the stars and sun were the color of Daddy's skin and the rest was tinted a faded blue. The word "ARMY" was tattooed in black under the chevron and the letters, "CBI" above. CBI stood for China-Burma-India, where Daddy served in the war.

He grabbed a dove and ran the large thumb of his right hand up underneath the breast of the bird and pulled the breast away from the back. I thought I heard the bird sigh. The stench of shit and heat and blood rose and he barked at me, "Come on now, Son. Get to cleaning before it gets dark."

I knew what to do. It was my job. I picked up a bird and ran my thumb under the breast. It was warm and moist in there. I pulled it away from the back. Something tore in there and then I stood with blood dripping onto my tennis shoes. The bird's wings were still attached to the breast.

He said, "The breast is the only part good to cook. It's really big in comparison to the rest of the bird." I'd heard all this before.

"Why, Daddy?"

"Because it flies a lot and it flies fast."

He stripped a membrane loaded with feathers off the meaty side of the breast. A little sack hung just below where the dove's head should have been. It was full of speckled spots, rusty-colored and yellow, too.

He pulled the sack off and the membrane broke and he pressed his thumb and forefinger together. I watched the tattoo of the veiled woman move. It looked like the veil swished from side to side. I giggled.

He asked, "What's so funny with that girly giggle?"

I said, "Nothing."

He nodded at the pile of dead birds. "Pay attention, now, Son."

It sounded like some white-wings flew back into the eucalyptus tree. I looked up and squinted into the last light.

Daddy grabbed my arm and yanked me around and spread the goo from the craw he busted onto the top of the ledge on the concrete tank.

"When a dove eats grain, they got no way, like humans, to digest it with the hulls of the grain so hard. So they get some gravel in their craw," he held up his right hand, "which I just busted here with my fingers." He smiled at me like I ought to be happy with that information. "Then they rattle that gravel around inside the craw and it breaks down the hulls on the grain so the birds can digest the food and get the nutrients." He held a piece of gravel between his thumb and forefinger.

I nodded. "What kind of nutrients, Daddy?"

He frowned and said, "We need to get back to cleaning these birds. You wash."

Water swished and swirled around the inside of the square concrete tank. It reminded me of the swimming pool in the park by our house.

Daddy busted the birds apart. The ones dead for a while stunk when he yanked the breasts away from the backs. He tossed the feathered backs in a pile at his feet and already the black ants were frenzied, moving in and out of the feathers and the guts, the hearts, the livers, the remains of the busted craws.

He pulled his sharp Case out of his pocket and used the small blade to snap the wings off. He threw these into the pile on top of the feathers and feet and guts and the black ants. Tiny gray and white feathers stuck to the tips of his fingers. He rubbed his fingertips on his trousers and left feathers and blood trails across his thighs.

I nodded at the spots. "Momma's going to get mad."

"Shut up and wash them dove breasts."

Sweat trickled into my left eye and stung. I grabbed a breast and leaned as far over the edge of the tank as I could and washed it. From the pipe on the left, hot water shot, and from the pipe on the other side, cold water. The cold and the hot washed up against my hands. I liked the way they felt, cold, then hot, cold then hot, and I began to swirl my hands through the water as I thought about the tattoo on his arm. The one with the veiled woman. I wondered if she was someone he knew. I wondered what my mother thought about it. I said, "Daddy, what does that ..."

"Shut up and quit playing around and get these birds washed. We need to get home and eat some supper."

"We going to eat these birds?"

"No time tonight, Son. I got to deliver gas tomorrow."

I put the breast I cleaned on the ledge and grabbed another. A Salem hung out of the left corner of Daddy's mouth. He reminded me of a bad guy in one of those old black-and-white movies he liked to watch with Humphrey Bogart or Jimmy Cagney. A thin pillar of smoke rose and must have burned his eye because he squinted and I saw his lips moving as if he was cussing under his breath. He does that at Momma, too.

I got another breast and washed it. I liked to scrub the feather and gut residue off in the hot water and rinse it with the cold. We worked pretty fast. I washed another one and then another, then I dropped one in the water.

"Goddamnit, Son. Pay the hell attention to what you're doing."

I flinched.

He bent over and reached into the water and grabbed

the dove breast off the gravel in the bottom of the tank. It was only a foot or two deep. When he pulled his arm out, water sheeted down his forearm and lit up the tattoo with the veil.

It reminded me of some old black and white pictures he had in a photo book he brought back from New Delhi with him. I wasn't alive then, but Momma said, "He brought them back from India." She frowned when she said that. Right after she said that, I thought I heard her crying. Her red face looked like the sky before one of those big dust storms we get.

In one of the pictures in the photo book, Daddy's sitting in a rickshaw with a dark-haired woman. He told me he worked with her and she was in the British Army. Both of them are smiling. Her teeth look long.

We packed the clean breasts in a Coleman ice chest and headed home. I don't think she's that pretty.

Big Thunder

As she charged off the patio into the back yard, I wondered what it was this time. She gripped the flyswatter—the orange one with the long, thin, metal-looped handle—in her right hand. She popped her chewing gum. I slowed the engine on the lawn mower. Sweat got in my eyes.

She yelled, "Boy, you're going to get it now."

I wiped the sweat with the front of my t-shirt. I said, "Why?"

She said, "You left those clothes in the washer and now they're sour."

"I forgot," I said.

Black thunderheads simmered over the top of the house. She swung that flyswatter. I heard it hiss.

She said, "You know your dad and I've been working ten or twelve hours a day. You need to help out."

I shrugged my shoulders.

She liked to bite her lower lip. She said, "Get over here, boy, and take your medicine."

I killed the engine on the lawn mower and started to walk over. I could taste the sweat dripping off my upper lip.

She looked like she wanted to swear. Something she rarely does. She said, "Get over here."

I said, "I am."

I thought about that sting and about taking the flyswatter away from her. Like last time. But the old man took his leather belt to me after that, left some ugly black-and-blue smears. Embarrassed me at the swimming pool.

I stopped in the middle of the back yard. She came at me, swinging the flyswatter in a low arc in front of her. I saw lightning flash, tightened my stomach in case it was real loud—the thunder, I mean.

She snapped me on the legs and I moved fast, got the mower between us. I could see a black widow in the end of the clothesline pole. Normally, I would have teased it some. My legs burned where she hit me. I looked down to see if I was marred. I planned on going swimming.

She said, "Get over here, boy. I'm going to put the fear of God in you."

She lurched, almost hit me again. I ran behind the picnic table. She ran around it, came at me. She was wearing shorts and one of those tops with the midriff missing. We went around the table. I didn't think she looked so hot, with her too-white skin and the way it rolled out the bottom of her top. Her outfit sported large red and yellow flowers of some kind. Nothing like that grew around here.

We stopped going around and around. She seethed as she stared at me, her breath short.

I couldn't see myself taking another switching. I said, "I reckon you better get on in the house."

Her eyebrows arched up as she laughed, "Or what?"

I said, "Or you'll regret it."

She snorted, "Isn't going to be like last time. You taking the swatter away from me. Your father took care of that."

I saw it in her eyes, hazel and mean. She wouldn't back off. There was lightning and thunder again, and again. It was loud. Made me want to cover my ears and run. Made me want to hide.

She chased me around the picnic table some more. I thought about leaving, but didn't have anywhere to go. All my friends' mothers would send me home. They stand together.

I winced at another blast of thunder. She laughed again, "See, already scaredy-cat, aren't you?"

I thought about the girls at the pool. I'd have to stay in the water all the time if I had any welts. They'd know why.

I looked at the picnic table as she stopped. Probably out of breath. I circled around so the table made a barrier between us again. As a flash of lightning severed the sky, I dropped on both knees and crawled under. The boom was so loud I gasped. I'm sure she did too, though I couldn't hear it. I stood up, the bulk of the table's weight on my neck and upper back. A burning smell pinched the air and raindrops the size of silver dollars started slapping the top of the table. I could see her lower legs and feet. I ran at her. I knew I should be afraid of my old man. She started running, too. I heard her Zory thongs slapping her soles. She screamed, "Your father's going to get you."

That made me laugh. I don't know why. Bursts of mirth jacked up my throat. I kept after her. She was getting away. I lifted my arms like I was doing military presses in the football room at high school. As my arms extended, I stopped running and catapulted the table after her. It missed by a mile. I heard the back door slam. The booms of big thunder and the smell of brimstone rocketed everywhere. I sprinted to the patio. Just before I got there, I noticed the flyswatter lying in the cut grass. I picked it up and threw it on the concrete beside the back door. I didn't want it out there in the yard, a hazard to me if the mower hit it. I had a vision of it going right through my heart.

I saw her moving around, watching me through the window. Probably locked the door. I grinned. I picked up the flyswatter and slapped the window three times, then walked to the edge of the patio. Lightning struck in the alley again. The blast hit me like a tackler. I flinched, but didn't cover my ears. I wanted the storm to stop. I was anxious to get to the swimming pool. She watched. I bet she was muttering under her breath, maybe even swearing.

Protean

I didn't get a letter from Amy even though I'd written her every day for the last month-and-a-half. I perched on the edge of my rack and used my footlocker for a desk and scrawled the words to another letter. I wondered if she even cared that I was going off to Nam to fight the war.

Instead of going out with the other guys to see *Bonnie and Clyde* in Oceanside, I finished the letter and then lounged around trying to fathom Volume I of Arnold J. Toynbee's *A Study of History*.

Walking by my rack on the way to the enlisted men's club, a stocky Wisconsin German, name of Dermer, stuck his face next to my head. "What are you reading that stupid shit for?"

I glared at Dermer, but the intensity of his blue-eyed stare forced me to retreat. No other answer came to mind, so I threw out, "I'm interested in it."

Dermer looked at Cline who waited behind. Dermer must have made a goofy face because Cline doubled over like he'd been shot by the funny gun.

Dermer went on, "You're just trying to look smarter than the rest of us."

I started to say, "I am smarter than the rest of you," but I didn't.

Dermer said, "If you weren't so much better than the rest of us, I'd take you to the club with me and Cline."

Dermer was twenty-one and could legally buy beer. I

nodded at Cline, "He isn't twenty-one."

Dermer laughed and Cline frowned. "Back home in Columbus, I pass for twenty-five."

He was probably right. He shaved three times a day to keep the lifers off his ass. His porcelain skin showed a dark mask three hours after he first put his safety razor to his face. I said, "Yeah, you pass for twenty-five, until you open your mouth."

Cline puffed up like a gunnery sergeant and hissed, "What's it to you, motherfucker?"

Dermer chuckled, "You two banty roosters calm down."

Cline punched Dermer's right shoulder, "Let's go get drunk."

I revisited Toynbee as they walked off. His words were long and dry and a lot of them seemed to jump off the page and insult my intelligence.

I heard Dermer and Cline walking down the hall, jive-assing about pitchers of Coors and Bud, Cline saying he didn't "like no western beer," and Dermer saying he'd prefer Strohs, too, but they'd take what they could get. The sound of the hard soles of their shoes on polished concrete echoed into the corners where the ceiling met the beige walls of the barracks.

I thought I understood, after reading three separate times, what Toynbee meant when he said, "... one peculiar feature of our age is the acceleration of the pace of change to an unprecedented degree as a result of 'the annihilation of distance' through the extraordinary recent advance of technology." I thought about the weapons we shot in training, and how they were different than in World War II and Korea; newer, easier to use.

And then I heard Dermer say, "You ought to put that brainy shit down and come to the club with me and Cline."

I looked at his square face. "You're sneaky. Crept right up on me."

He nodded and smiled.

I said, "I'm not twenty-one and I don't think Cline wants me there."

He laughed. "As long as you don't try to buy beer, the lifers don't care. You're a trained killer for Christ's sake. They'll sell it to me and you need to stop being so worried about how other people see you."

I tossed the book down on my rack and sat up and looked at him. "But the law says you have to be twenty-one."

"Fuck the law." He threw his arms out wide like Perry Como.

I explained, "We haven't had mail call yet today."

He chuckled. "And we ain't going to have it this late in the day. Besides, it's Friday night."

He reached down and grabbed the front of my utility jacket and yanked me close. "Forget that little sugar puss you think's at home in love with you. She's just like you left her, but now she's in the back seat of some other guy's GTO fucking his legs off."

I grabbed his wrist with my right hand and tried to loosen his grip. I aimed a punch with my left, but he turned his head and I missed. He laughed as he shoved me back. "Okay for you, if you want to pine about old sugar puss, but if you think you want to get drunk with your warrior buddies, I'll let you drink with us."

My face felt like the barrel of a rifle too hot to touch. He grinned at me while he walked away. "Don't forget, if you decide to come, you got to wear your dress khaki uniform with a tie and spit-shined shoes to get in the club on Friday night."

"Fuck you," I whispered.

I picked up Toynbee and read, "History is now being made so fast that it is constantly taking us by surprise."

I thought, what the fuck does he mean by that? I put the book on my lap and closed my eyes and tried to think about history:

1. Caesar and Cleopatra sailing down the Tiber River
2. Charles Martel smashing the Saracens at Tours
3. Henry II locking Eleanor in the tower
4. Oliver Cromwell massacring Catholics at Drogheda
5. Pancho Villa invading Columbus, New Mexico

But at every instance, Amy's face popped up instead. Well, not really her face, but more an image of her being. I wanted her face. Her blond hair, her green eyes and the full lips that sometimes seemed too full. But I couldn't capture that image. All I could grab hold of was something more like misty hints, words she'd said to me here and there. Especially phrases like, "I love you."

I slammed Toynbee against the wall. The book slapped and pages fluttered as it fell to the deck. A phone rang in the duty office. I sat up and tried to see her without any clothes, her small breasts, the rust-red nipples, her thin waist and gymnast's thighs. I heard the officer of the day stomp into the duty office bitching about the dirty squad bay. Amy had her eyes closed and her full lips just barely parted. The officer of the day started yelling at the duty NCO.

I picked up Toynbee and thumbed through the eared pages. I found my place as I sat on the floor by my rack so the officer of the day couldn't discover me. Toynbee went on:

"The second peculiar feature of our age is that the past has become doubly protean." I thought, what the hell does "protean" mean? I opened my footlocker and found my *Webster's* and looked up the word.

1. readily assuming different forms or characters; extremely variable
2. changeable in shape or form, as an amoeba
3. (of an actor or actress) versatile; able to play many kinds of roles
4. of, pertaining to, or suggestive of Proteus

I wasn't sure what all that meant. Again I tried to dig up a good mental look at Amy's naked body on the back seat of my daddy's Buick Riviera.

The officer of the day screamed, "Why is all this mail still on this desk?"

The duty NCO said, "I wasn't supposed to be on duty tonight, so I ..."

"Get this mail out to these Marines as soon as possible. They're all going to Nam next week."

My face felt hot as I thought, why the hell didn't he give me my mail? I decided to march up to the duty office and demand it.

As I approached, the duty officer yelled, "But first, secure a bunch of Marines and get this squad bay policed up."

I didn't want to spend the whole night cleaning shitters that didn't need cleaning and buffing an already shiny deck. I ducked down the long barracks back to my rack and hiding Toynbee beneath my pillow, changed into my khaki gabardine trousers and long-sleeve shirt, a tie and the rest of the uniform required for me to get into the club, including my newly spit-shined shoes.

I marched across the asphalt grinder that separated the barracks from the PX, the chow hall and the club.

I heard Cline's hard Ohio vernacular and figured he was already lit up pretty good. I wondered how fast they'd been drinking. He saw me and giggled, "Well, here comes old sugar puss lover."

Dermer turned and opened his arms. He said, "Alright, my man decided to stop pining about the pussy."

Cline shouted, "And quit worrying about getting smart."

Dermer slapped him on the chest with the back of his big hand. "Keep it down. If you get too stupid they'll throw you out."

The bar was dark and only five or six tables were occupied. Dermer grabbed an empty glass and sloshed it full of beer. There wasn't much of a head on it so I figured it would taste flat, but I didn't want to end up policing the barracks, so I picked it up.

Dermer grinned. The way the light glinted I really noticed the gap between his incisors. "I expected you," he said.

His smug expression bugged me. I swigged the whole glass of flat beer and slammed the empty on the table.

Cline snapped to attention and saluting me, shouted that characteristic Marine Corps "Aoorah!"

Dermer poured me another glass and said, "Let's celebrate. We'll be going to war in a week."

I took another long drink and felt a squiggle at the base of my brain.

Cline snapped to attention again and announced, "To health, women, war and conquest."

Dermer grinned and looked at me. "Forget about that dumb-assed pussy you pine about."

I shook my head and looked away. A golden neon light in the window read "Coors," and a red one in the other window advertised "Budweiser."

Cline was talking about Ohio State's basketball team and how well they played and Dermer marched off to get another pitcher and I wondered why Amy wouldn't write me and then Dermer was back, his long, strong left arm around my shoulders hugging me as he filled all three glasses again. I started to get some money out of my pocket and he said, "No. It's all on me."

For some reason my eyes teared up and as I turned away Cline yelled, "Aoorah!"

Dermer whispered, "Lookee here, you got to forget that bitch. She's screwing your best buddy right now."

I shook my head so hard my brain banged against the inside of my skull. I took another swallow of beer but I threw the glass up to my mouth so fast the beer sloshed around the corners, ran down my chin and onto my neck, my chest, and the table.

"Aoorah!"

Dermer chuckled. "Think of all that pussy out there just waiting for you to fuck them. All ... them ... women."

Cline screamed, "Women."

Dermer slapped him on the chest again, but harder as he said to me, "Can't handle his brew."

Cline whimpered, "I'm sorry, I'll behave." His eyes seemed teary, too. "Let's talk about the war."

Dermer threw his arms out. "Why?"

Cline cringed, "Because I'm scared and nobody talks about being scared."

I announced, "War is protean."

Dermer giggled as Cline said, "What the fuck's that mean?"

My head spun as Dermer headed for another pitcher. I nodded to Cline, "Protean—think about it like this. War changes. Think of the weapons we've got. Not like those old grunts at Belleau Wood and Iwo and Chosin Reservoir. It should be a lot easier for us."

I felt Dermer back at my shoulder as Cline said, "Do you think it's going to be easy?"

I shook my head, "No. I said easier."

Cline nodded.

Dermer said, "Easier? What?"

Cline grinned and stood at attention and snapped, "Easier. This war. Our war is protean and shall be easier."

Dermer looked at the table. He raised his eyebrows. "Fucking easier? You'll both be lucky if you don't get your asses blown away." He filled our glasses again as Cline marched off to hunt for the head and even though it seemed like we'd just arrived, the bartender kept yelling, "Last call," and Dermer hissed, "Here, let's finish this so I can get us another before they close."

Cline staggered back singing the Marine Corps Hymn.

Dermer rolled his eyes at me.

Cline's voice broke. "Here is health to you and to our

Corps, whom we are proud to serve."

I went to find the head, too, and as I rounded a corner I heard Cline's song chasing me, "In many a strife we fought for life and never lost our nerve."

I had to put my hand against the wall as I took a leak in the urinal. It stunk and made my stomach rumble. I felt piss stick to the soles of my spit-shined shoes.

Outside the head, Marines vacated the club. I tried to walk in a straight line as I marched back to our table. A full pitcher of beer sat waiting my arrival and I said, "We don't have time to drink that."

Dermer said, "We ain't Marines if we can't kill that," as he sloshed our glasses full. We swilled them down, then another and another as the hands on the clock that hung on the wall read 1:45, 1:53, 2:00.

Outside, Cline shot vomit onto the asphalt grinder. The stench hit me where my belt buckled and beer rocketed up my esophagus and burned my throat and mouth and nose.

Dermer said, "You two are a real bunch of pussies."

Cline yelled, "It's protean. Aoorah! Forward march."

And we stepped out marching on line as Cline called cadence, "Yo la-o ri la-o, yo la-o ri la-o, you'll never get back to your life, yo la-o ri la-o, and Jodie is fucking your wife, yo la-o ri la-o, right oblique, hunh, the world is full of strife, yo la-o ri la-o, and Jodie's still fucking your wife, yo la-o ri la-o, sound off, one two, sound off, three four, sound off, one, two, three, four! Three, four!" And we marched like we were Boots on the grinder at Marine Corps Recruit Depot, the heels of our spit-shined shoes striking the deck at precisely the same moment.

Four-hundred yards of asphalt intervened between us and our barracks. A line of skimpy pines flanked our left and to our right a lone streetlight shot wan beams in a circle on the edge of the grinder. A few early-season moths flitted and battered at the light. I saw the barracks far ahead through blurry vision. Light escaped from the duty office and advanced toward us as we advanced towards it. Cline yelled, "There's a pillbox full of gooks up ahead. They got a fifty-caliber machine gun. Ba-boomp, ba-boomp, ba-boomp."

Dermer slapped him across the chest and stared in the direction Cline pointed. "Let's take that fucker out. I'll lay down a base of fire. You two Marines advance ten meters and then you lay down a base of fire while I advance and when I gets there, me and Maloney," he slapped me across the chest, "will advance another ten meters. We keep that up 'til we get close enough to drop a grenade in on them fuckers."

Cline yelled, "Aye, aye, Private First Class Dermer," as he and I crouched low and rushed ahead, our make-believe M-16s at our shoulders. Cline made rifle fire sounds. "Sht-titititit. Shitititit. Sling-ang. Shititititit!"

I yelled, "Incoming," and hit the deck and as I did the asphalt bit into the knees of my gabardine trousers. For a moment I returned to the real world and saw lifers in my face yelling about the shape of my gear.

Cline continued with the sound effects of make-believe gunfire. The light from the duty office seemed a lot closer. Through the window I noticed someone, maybe the officer of the day, reading something. I knew he was reading my mail from Amy.

Cline yelled, "Let's get them pukes. It's protean."

Dermer hit the deck next to me. He looked at Cline and said, "What the fuck does that mean?"

Cline yelled, "I don't fucking know. I just like the way it sounds."

Dermer slapped me on the back and said, "Let's advance." I got on my knees. I sensed the toes of my spit-shine shoes grate on the grinder. One of my knees felt like a knife had been jammed into the cap. Cline made war sounds, "Varoom," and, "Rat-a-tat-tat."

As I advanced on the enemy, I screamed, "Stop reading

my fucking mail."

Dermer yelled, "What mail, you fucking nut? We're in a firefight."

I whispered, "The lieutenant's reading my love letters."

Dermer scoffed, "You don't know what love is."

"Yes I do. I love her. I love her. I LOVVVVE HERRRRR."

He knelt down and then jerked me down, too. I felt something wet running down my leg from the aching kneecap. I tried to look down and see what it was, but Dermer grabbed my upper arm and squeezed. My biceps burned. Dermer hissed, "Listen to me you crazy fuck. You ain't in love. Just think about all that pussy out there. Think about what you're going to be like if you survive the war. A fucking stud. Think about all that pussy out there just waiting for a man like you."

I looked at Dermer who stared at the objective. He ground his teeth and squinted. I glanced at where the barracks were supposed to be. The lights in the duty office were off. Everything out there looked black. Blood dripped and crept like a spider on my leg.

Routine

A rush of rapids gouged the morning. Songbirds twitted and bees buzzed. Trees jutted, limbs thick. Small glints of sunshine on water here and there. Sweat ran down my back, my feet burned. New boots. I wanted to drop my flak jacket, my helmet and rifle, strip naked and jump into the river. But we patrolled.

Every other morning, the five of us on patrol. The fire team and Sergeant Swank. I brought up the rear. Newest grunt. Spent a lot of time trying to walk backwards, protecting the ass-end of the patrol.

Sergeant Swank called me Ass-end. He said, "Your job's to keep the ass-end of the patrol from getting hit. Don't worry your little butt none about what happens up front."

He always said through his perfect white teeth, "Gooks smell different. We smell like soap. And C-ration beef. Lucky Strikes and heat tabs. Learn the signs. The scents."

So, listening for a cough, a whisper. Lifting my nose into the air just like Sergeant Swank. Trying to smell cheap tobacco, firewood, dried fish.

I tried to walk backwards. I heard birds croak. Looked like a scorcher, maybe a hundred degrees and humidity. Rain in the evening. And mosquitoes.

I heard Swank talk on the radio to the platoon commander. Sounded like squelch, "Negative activity, over."

The river roared as it scrabbled over rough rocks. High banks channeled it along. I stared into the riffles that sparkled like winking whores in Danang.

Past the rapids the sound of the river almost died. Some large white birds lifted off from a dead tree on the opposite bank. They croaked as their huge wings labored. As if to sound an alarm, they circled and squawked.

I thought I heard laughter. Faint, as the river skittered over rocks. Like children on the playground, kickball and monkey bars. Made sense to me. Sergeant Swank said children from the villes on the other side of the river came and bathed their water buffaloes. "Those Viet Cong villes," as he called them.

I felt sweat trickle down the inside of my right leg as I held my rifle at high port, safety off, nose in the air. I kept my eyes to the rear of the patrol.

Sergeant Swank always said, "When gooks are around, something unnatural will pop up. Fresh turned dirt, crushed leaves. Branches that don't belong on a tree. The scent of gook cigarettes. Pay attention."

I smelled the morning, moss and mold, damp air, odor of bovine critters, fecal matter, flowers I did not know.

I looked around for snapped branches, broken stems.

Suddenly a burst of gunfire, then yelling. I turned but the patrol was farther down the trail. I couldn't see what sounded like bedlam. Screaming like women. I crouched and scrabbled in a duck walk toward the action. My thigh muscles burned. The river widened, now a thousand yards, surface flat and thin with stones stubbing the surface. Across the river water buffaloes scattered, feet kicking, horned heads thrown about like great spears. I heard what sounded like laughing children. Swank and the rest of the team sprayed the far bank with rifle fire. Doone launched an M-79 grenade; knocked small limbs into the canopy.

Swank yelled, "Cease fire."

Quiet again. The only sounds, men breathing like they'd been sprinting, my boot soles scuffing the bank as I ap-proached Swank. My heart pounding. The scent of spent gunpowder invaded my nose. Not fish or firewood.

Swank squinted at me, "Get any, Ass-end?"

I said, "Any what?"

He said "Gooks."

"I wasn't shooting."

"Why the fuck not?"

His perfect white teeth gleamed in the sunlight.

I nodded towards the far bank and said, "Those sounded like kids to me."

Somebody laughed. Swank said, "This is the way it is, Ass-end. Little gooks grow up to be big gooks."

Everybody laughed. Doone reloaded his M-79. Upstream the white birds landed in the dead tree.

Running into Chief

Pure hell. The gooks pre-targeted the gates. Knew their shit. I don't remember much except that going outside the wire seemed like leaping into a bonfire. Waiting for the blast of burn and then death. I remember crawling, my elbows like oars rowing in the red mud. No trees, no cover, just red mud for a quarter of a mile.

I knew the country well. Before they blew hell out of it. Now splintered trunks of murdered trees. Shell craters. I ran bent like I had a swivel at my waist. Grenades hanging off my front yanking me into the ground. I heard the scream-bash-flying-whine of shrapnel. Several times, knocked to my knees. Sound banging in my ears. Sweat under my helmet. Mouth like sandpaper.

Second Platoon walked into an ambush. Heading out to rescue them. Heard chatter over the radio, screaming, shrieking, men yelling, calling medevacs and artillery strikes. Ambushed. Charlie pounding our asses, making a quarter of a mile and a rescue attempt a death trap. Had some plans, old Charlie did.

All that incoming separated us. Instead of our three squads, just a bunch of men. I heard rifle fire up ahead. The swoosh of rockets and some yelling. We weren't a unit. Just a bunch of men trying to salvage Second Platoon. I looked back and saw the base camp. It sat up there, angry on the red hill, its barbwire barrier thick. Reminded me of swarms of bees that lived in this land. Not like our good old docile USA bees. Gook bees were hostile.

I got a sense of where we were. Knew where Second Platoon was supposed to be. Over the next ridge south.

Moon and I managed to progress up to the old road that ran out to Route Nine, alongside it a ditch. We rolled in, breathing hard. Noise roiled the air, rumbled along in great waves that shook the ground. Made it hard to talk. We shouted.

Moon said, "Where the hell you think they are?"

In the ditch, two Marines from Second Platoon. I yelled at them, "Where they at?"

They looked at me. Dazed. One of them was bleeding from both ears. Shell shock and no control. They both shook. One had pissed his pants.

I yelled, "Where the hell's Second Platoon Commander?"

The one with blood coming out his ears chuckled, "What commander?"

I looked at Moon, "Let's move."

He said, "Let's take them with us."

I shrugged.

Moon said, "Come on, Marines, we got a war to fight."

They stared at us, their mouths open.

I prodded one, then the other with the end of my rifle. "Come on, let's beat feet. We got to get your comrades."

The one who'd pissed his pants lowered his head and slumped in the red mud. The man with blood coming out his ears nodded and said, "Affirmative, let's move out."

I said, "You lead out?"

He nodded.

We lit out and left the other man blubbering. On up the ditch a couple of hundred yards, the sound of machine gun rattle-bang-palaver snapping off the sides of the blood-colored hills. Over the road and up a rise, then at the top on our bellies and looking in a draw and bodies lying scattered, and up the other side of the draw gooks popping out of a fresh-dug trench. Behind them I could see bodies of our guys. I knew the score. Got suckered right in. Then shot from behind. Chicken shit way to fight. Fucking gooks.

Down in the draw, in groups of twos and threes, Marines fired back, charging around getting shot and plopping on the ground. At the lowest part of the draw, a creek and some green bushes, two trees and behind them seven or eight Marines, some firing, others tending to wounded. I nodded at Moon who, with the other Marine, took off as I sprayed the gook trench line with rifle fire, full automatic; how sweet the feeling.

Moon and the Marine with blood oozing out his ears ran about seventy-five yards and then they were in the bottom of the draw. Mortars started dropping around me. I felt the rounds walking my way. I rolled over the top and half ran, half slithered in the mud. It got in my nose and eyes. I couldn't stop. I heard rifle rounds snap by my head. I kept down, couldn't see to do anything but dredge my way to some place where the mayhem might stop. Mud in my nostrils, mud in my eyes. The clay grains grated, tears welled up. Blinded me. Irritated. Needed to see, to fire my rifle. There were targets out there, but I couldn't acquire them. I needed to kill somebody. Frustrating.

At the bottom of the draw, Moon was giving orders. I chuckled. He wanted to run everything. I started to countermand but then saw Chief. Oklahoma Indian ... Kiowa? Choctaw? Apache? All three? Every Indian in the Marine Corps is named Chief. He'd been in all the big fire fights.

Chief kneeled over a trembling body with a bloody crotch. Chief with his acne-pocked face, little craters like smallpox. I let Moon take command. He established fields of fire and called in artillery strikes. I heard the scream of jets streaking. I thought, we'll get out of this. Lots of firepower brought down on this place. Overkill, goddamnit. Any kind of kill to make them stop; fucking gooks.

Chief held the bleeding man's hands and talked softly.

I said, "Chief, what's going on?"

He said, "Wiped out. The whole damned platoon up there behind all those gooks, the platoon sergeant, the right guide. Just us left."

I said, "Moon, round them up and get them out of here."

"What about the KIAs?"

"Just get the wounded out."

"Aye, aye."

I looked at the lieutenant, twenty-one and bleeding to death. I looked at his crotch, some of the blood dry, some big green flies.

Chief said, "Got it in the balls. Shitty place to buy it."

The lieutenant screamed. Didn't look so squared away like he did the day he came in-country. Now his face stretched tight, his body arched like he was wrestling.

Chief said, "Hold on, Sir. We got a medevac coming right away."

I looked at Chief, "There's no way we'll get a chopper ..."

As he shrugged he put his hand over my mouth.

I started to say, "Don't try to shut me up," but instead I said, "Moon, get them moving while this black smoke obscures the field."

I nodded at Chief. He grabbed the lieutenant's shoulders and lifted. The lieutenant screamed like bayonets stabbed his guts.

I yelled, "Move it out. Stay in formation. Somebody help Chief."

The Marine with blood running out his ears grabbed Chief's weapon and the lieutenant's, too. Little pools of blood had accumulated where the lieutenant had been. Reminded me of the desert at home, recesses in rocks after cloudbursts. Up our side of the draw and incoming knocking us down, the lieutenant screaming and Chief like an old mule. Nothing bothered him, just kept moving his wide shoulders and his steady feet.

At the gate the man stopped screaming. Chief put him down like placing young kittens at the nipples of their mammy. The lieutenant's face like yellow wax. His eyes black and gazing straight into the afternoon sun.

Chief sat and put his head between his knees. Moon knelt beside me and we looked back at the road and the ditch and beyond to the ridges where the remains of those other Marines still lay. Nobody left out there. Not really. Just incoming, geysers of red earth and flying shrapnel.

Riley

A few clicks down the river, we veered off to the west into a wide, flat plain with rice paddies as far as you could see. Dikes rose with banana-looking plants at their bases. Little high points sat cloaked in the shadows of tall trees, undergrowth. I kept my eye on these places ... the dikes, the high spots.

The heat beat us like eggs frying on a griddle. My canteens were heavy. I wanted to sit down and drain them. I needed discipline to get me through this day. I downed some salt tablets, licked my lips as we swept through the paddies.

We reconned a tree line by fire. Some wing-wiper flying by thought he saw movement. We lit the day up with tracers and M-79 blasts, the crash and rattle of gunfire a welcome change from the tired old routine. I burnt three magazines. We sent a rifle team in to sweep the trees. No sign but old sign, they reported. The lieutenant nodded.

We turned north and entered territory I'd never been in. I couldn't recognize anything although Sergeant Slade assured me he'd been there plenty of times, but, as he also assured me, he wasn't a boot-ass like me; had been in-country a lot longer. I wasn't sure I believed him. About being out there before, that is.

The rice paddies seemed different. Had a different color. Red like dry rust. And there were low hills off towards the river. I heard monkeys and the vegetation was greener.

More lush.

We occupied a high point in a large rice paddy. We set up a perimeter and the lieutenant called the squad leaders to his command post. I could hear them talking, but didn't understand. I smoked a Lucky. Heat shimmered off the hardpan paddy. The waves in the air danced off towards what looked like another deserted ville a couple of thousand meters to my front. The day sat quiet in the heat. Catching its breath.

After the parley with the lieutenant, Slade came over to me and said, "You're on point."

He smiled at me. He never smiled at me. He nodded at the ville off across the paddy. "That's our objective. Get over there and take your fire team in. Run your flankers out to the edge of the tree line. I'll assign you an extra two men to check the rest of the place out." He gritted his teeth when he looked off across the paddy. "We'll follow you in."

I stared at the ville. Didn't like the cut of the place. Seemed like a fortress out there on its own.

Slade said, "You got that?"

I said, "Aye, aye."

He said, "You got a problem with that?"

I said, "No."

I might have had a problem with it. Seemed alien out there. Isolated. But what the hell, the old Marine saying, "Ours is not to question why. Ours is but to do or die."

I told Riley and my other men to saddle up. They grumbled, looked gaunt in their sweaty jungle dungarees.

We crossed the paddy in a two-column formation with my team up front, the five of us spread out in the shape of an arrowhead with me right behind the center. I wanted to get there as fast as possible. To get the shit over if any existed.

The lieutenant wanted to go slower. He yelled, "Slow it down up there."

I looked at my men, met their eyes. We were of the same

mind. Why slow it down if you're going to meet your destiny?

We covered the distance between our take-five and the ville in what seemed like no time. Oh sure, the time is the same, I reckon, but when you're hunting for Charlie and you think you might find him, things seem to swoop past you, rushing confrontation at you as you smell the dirt in the paddy, the dried and rotten rice roots, some fecal matter from a bird, the faint scent of unknown flowers.

The ville sat in a grove of large trees and had six or seven masonry buildings around. Barns and storehouses, I reckoned. The main house's roof was caved in. Reminded me of the ribcage of some long-dead bovine critter. I slowed the patrol and stepped out front, then walked to each man and told him to stay ten meters from the man on either flank and move through to the other side. Encounter a building, search it. Try to stay in eye contact. I told Riley to follow me. We'd search the old house.

The lieutenant said, "Go slow."

I said, "Aye, aye."

Under my breath I said, "Fuck you." If it's there, let's find it.

I moved out and the team stayed on line. The walls of the ville were a faded gray. We hadn't seen the enemy since I'd been in-country. Mildew stains were like splatted chow on the chipped plaster. If Charlie was around, we'd have seen him by now, had a firefight. I entered through a large opening where huge double doors had hung. They were now on the floor. I thought I heard a scraping sound. A slight breeze got up and flitted through the treetops. I thought I heard the squawk of a peacock. The breeze blowing against my sweaty back chilled me. It made me nervous, having the wind to my back. Won't be able to use my smeller, I thought. Wind affects your ability to hear. I thought I heard a scraping sound again. Slade appeared at my side. His eyes got large and round. He nodded at me. Riley was nowhere to be seen.

I stepped off towards the large room where I thought I heard the scraping sound. I lifted my feet high, trying to limit my own noise. Yellow plaster lay on the floor in large pieces. The scraping sound again. I lifted my rifle to my shoulder, looked through the peep sight as I stepped along. Rat turds came into focus. I heard Slade behind me. I thought, stupid fuck. Stay still. I glared at him. He stopped, glared back as if shouting.

I heard the scraping again, decided to go in on full automatic. I flipped the selector on my weapon. When I did, it sounded as if I'd clanged a wrench on the side of a tank. I took a deep breath and charged. Movement in the corner of my left eye caused me to pull the trigger. The report of my first burst rattled around the inside of the old building. I thought I heard a cry of fear. Plaster and dust flew off the walls. The stench of gunpowder burned my nose. I looked at the movement in the corner of my eye as I worked the muzzle of my weapon in that direction.

I saw a clump of dirty white cloth on the floor. Vietnamese newspapers lay scattered about. The letters looked like characters from an art show. The white clump moved. I sensed no danger, stopped firing, pointed my rifle at the clump.

Slade screamed, "Keep firing. Kill him. Kill it."

I watched the clump. It moved. I started to pull the trigger, but stopped. The clump moved again. What must have been a head looked up. The face was mostly covered in gossamer fabric.

Slade screamed, "Nail that fucking thing, or I will." He came next to me, his rifle at his shoulder. I grabbed the barrel of his weapon and pulled it down.

"Knock it off, Slade."

The thing moved its head as if watching us. I could see spotted, scabbed skin through the gaps in the cloth. It turned my stomach.

Slade said, "I'm giving you an order, Lance Corporal. Kill

it, or let me."

I could smell the thing, wondered if it, he, she, was a former owner of this place, or a hired hand, or just an opportunist, hiding from the craziness. The stench nauseated. I looked at Slade, pushed the barrel of his rifle against his leg, said, "Fuck you, Sergeant. I con't kill sick things. We don't shoot sick things."

Slade turned his mouth down in a sneer, tried to pull the barrel of his rifle up. I pushed harder, moved up against his body. We stood close, our faces locked in combat.

"As you were." The voice startled me. I looked. It was the lieutenant. His radioman stood behind. The radio antenna whipped, whished.

The lieutenant looked at the thing in the dingy white cloth, then at us. "As you were, Marines. Let's move out. Only a leper. Let him be, he can't do us any harm."

I released Slade's rifle barrel. He hissed, "Fucking maggot. I'll get you for this."

I looked at the thing. It moved its head slightly as if it were assessing me. I stared at the floor, walked outside, looked for Riley. Wanted to know why he hadn't got my back.

Norwegian Wood

On the flight from Khe Sanh to Phu Bai no rockets hit the big chopper, no sniper rounds from an AK-47, no machine gun bullets through the thin metal bottom to mangle my legs—just misty morning with thick forests and April-green rice paddies floating beneath as we sped southeast. Large white birds flew below us.

I tried to think about Leanna. I hadn't received a letter from her in months. But I wasn't alone. Mail up on the plateau was sparse. Maybe the mail burned up with one of the choppers that got hit in the Tet Offensive or maybe the pogues in the battalion mailroom were running behind. Maybe a letter from Leanna awaited me in Phu Bai right then.

After we landed, I located First Battalion Rear and checked in at the transient barracks. The doofus lieutenant in charge sported utilities like the kind we wore stateside, new and starched. I started to laugh but he cut me a severe glance through thick black-rimmed glasses and ordered, "Get your butt down to the chow hall and eat, then go turn your weapon in."

I liked the idea of some hot chow after months of short rations and C-rats.

I said, "Aye, aye, Sir."

He sneered, "If you need directions, report to the corporal at the desk in the next office."

I stopped at the corporal's desk. He glanced at me like

I was dirt. Must have been the ripped and dust-imbedded utilities I'd worn since January. I glowered back. He gave me directions to the chow hall and the battalion supply depot.

I started to walk out of his office but turned back. "I didn't get a lot of mail up on the plateau."

He said, "Maybe nobody loves you."

"I don't think you pogues sent it up there."

He didn't answer, just stared. He finally said, "What makes you think so?"

I shrugged. "Like I said, Corporal, I haven't had much since January."

He shook his head. My stomach erupted into a burn and I had to ball my fists to keep from grabbing him by the front of his fancy clean utility jacket and shaking him. I thought about Leanna instead, her shoulder-length blonde hair with the flip, her muscled calves, her cheerleader's leap with full splits.

I said, "Is there some way I can get my mail?"

"You best forget it."

I didn't want to forget it. Or Leanna's face, or my mother's chocolate chip cookies which were probably spoiled by now. And Leanna's thin nose with the little knot about halfway down.

Up there on the plateau, I'd imagine her tongue tangled inside my mouth. That helped keep all those rocket and artillery attacks jammed into a separate mental compartment; that and what I'd do with her when I got her away from her severe mother, her dad. That's what kept me from going nuts up there.

I said, "I don't want to forget about it."

He turned and looked out the window to his rear. There wasn't anything out that window but another hut like the one I was standing in. He drummed his clean fingers on his desk and grunted. He sucked his lower lip between his teeth. He sighed, "Okay, Marine. I'll see what I can do."

I said, "How soon, Corporal? I'm anxious."

He squinted at me. "Check in after chow."

I nodded.

On the way to chow I thought about having to turn my weapon in. I didn't like being stripped of my means of self-defense. What would I do if the gooks burst through the wire?

As I entered the chow hall, the other Marines stared at my old utility jacket. The smell of fresh-cooked food made my stomach grumble. Somebody laughed and I wondered if it was at me. I looked pretty damned ragged. My jungle boots were coming apart, my helmet cover stained with red mud.

Gooks served the food, a couple of short, old men and some young girls all wearing black uniforms with white aprons. Take those aprons off, I thought, and they could be Charlie, waiting to ambush us.

The last time I'd been down here, in the fall of '67, I ate at a PX. Maybe I should go find it and get a cheeseburger, but then I figured gooks probably worked there, too.

I looked around the chow hall and noticed a lot of Marines chowing down on roast beef and mashed potatoes with what smelled like real meat gravy, and white bread and vegetables and milk and coffee and desserts of all kinds. My stomach growled and hurt, so I stuffed my reluctance and got a tray.

The gooks in the chow line smiled at me but I kept my eyes down as they shoveled me food. I wondered why they wasted the effort of faking how they really felt. I found a place to sit among a bunch of office pogues. I had to glare to force one of them to move over and make a place for me at the end of the long trestle table. As I sat down I noticed all their clean fingernails and scrubbed faces.

One of them, a sergeant, said, "Who you with up there on the plateau?"

"Bravo, Second Platoon."

"Saw a lot of shit, huh?"

My mouth full of mashed potatoes and gravy, I nodded.

He said, "You know McCarthy?"

"No."

He smiled at me, but I kept shoveling it in as fast as I could. All the Marines chowing down plus the gooks in the serving line made tasty targets. Incoming would blast a hole in the wall and maim all of us. Could happen any minute. Would be a good time for it. Nobody paying attention.

The sergeant said, "McCarthy and I were in supply school together. But after we got here, he volunteered to be a grunt."

"That so?"

"Yeah, crazy, huh?"

I flicked my eyes up at him. He smiled again and looked at the men sitting around. They all laughed.

Then somebody let out a goofy high-pitched giggle. Reminded me of Leanna's laugh.

I said, "Yeah, crazy."

The sergeant asked me about some other Marines up there, but I hadn't heard of them, so I didn't respond. That laugh made me think about Leanna and my stereo and my records hidden under her bed. My Beatles collection, all my Stones albums. I wanted her to get a lot of enjoyment out of them while I was over here nearly dying for my don't-give-a-shit fellow Americans. Before I left the States to come over to Nam, I told her she could listen to them if she took good care. Her and nobody else.

I stuffed my gullet until I thought I'd pop—slabs of roast beef and gravy, green beans, apple crisp, hot rolls crammed with pats of butter. I drank a lot of water to help get the chow down my throat as fast as possible before an incoming artillery round crashed through the roof and killed us all.

After I finished I belched real loud and again that high-pitched, goofy giggle caught me by surprise—just like Leanna's. I wondered what she was doing for fun. Some lifer major glared at me from the officer's mess. We had a little staring contest and when he turned and resumed eating, I went back to thoughts of Leanna and her having fun and with whom. I hadn't had a letter in a long time.

Later, back at the battalion transient barracks, the corporal had a pile of mail bundled inside a thick rubber band. He said, "There might be more. This was all I could locate."

I said, "Much thanks."

He nodded.

Outside I thumbed through the envelopes. All but one were from my mother. I tossed those into the shit can beside the door of the hut.

The letter I kept was from one of Leanna's friends. A friend of mine, too. Jinny. Sometimes I dated Jinny when Leanna and I were on the fritz. When I wanted to piss Leanna off. Jinny was horny for me but every time we tried to get intimate it was like I had one too many tongues and not enough hands. I guessed that meant I was for Leanna.

I sniffed the letter to see if there was any perfume on it. It smelled like paper and red dust. Noticing the postmark, I thought, not that long ago, ten days, pretty fresh news.

I folded the letter in half and slipped it in the front pocket of my utility jacket and walked down to the armory to turn in my weapon. The red land was scuffed where slit-trenches and fighting holes gouged the ground and a bright sun lit up the faded green sandbags that buttressed every bunker and wall. Mighty-Mites and six-bys ran up and down the dusty roads. Red grit hung in the afternoon. A lot of Marines in fresh green utilities walked the streets, their faces flush like happy children. They looked well fed and a lot of them carried on with a saltier-than-you attitude. Some carried clean, black weapons, mostly .45 caliber side-arms, while others wandered around unarmed, grab-assing like there wasn't a war going on outside.

I found Battalion Supply. A lot of busy supply clerks milled between shelves stacked high with all kinds of gear and I wondered where clean web cartridge belts had been when we needed them, and the jungle boots, the cases of C-rations, camouflage utilities and helmet covers. I thought, I bet those have been here all along. Wonder why they weren't sent up to the plateau where the fighting was going on. Maybe all the scuttlebutt was true, gear being traded to the Vietnamese for pot and cheap booze.

I stopped at a counter and whistled at a corporal studying a mess of papers. He glanced at me. I nodded for him to come but he just sneered and went back to studying his papers. I stuck the thumb and forefinger of my right hand in between my lips and whistled again, creating a high-pitched shriek that I was confident made everybody's ears sting. A bunch of other supply pogues gave me an alarmed glance. I took half a step back. I didn't like all those eyes watching me.

The focus of my whistle stalked over and demanded. "What d'ya need, Marine?" He had green eyes. The same as Leanna.

I said, "The armory."

He glared towards a long hall and then pointed his index finger like a pistol. I nodded.

He yelled, "You're welcome," as I walked away. I shot him the bird but not so he could see me.

When I found the armory I recognized one of the Marines working there. He'd been in our platoon before the shit hit the fan on the plateau. He looked well fed, too. So did the other Marine working with him. I assumed the one I didn't know was the assistant because he was cleaning an M-60 machine gun while my acquaintance was reading a fuck book. I couldn't remember my acquaintance's name, but I recalled his face, his short blond hair, brown eyes spaced too far apart, a square jaw and a regular-Joe nose. He looked at me and smiled. "Adams."

His hair was the color of Leanna's.

I wondered how he remembered my name. "Yeah, it's me."

"Rotating home?"

"I'm gone."

He nodded and pointed a thumb behind without looking, "This is Jake."

Jake sported short dark hair highlighting a delicate white face. No circles ringed his eyes like the faces I'd stared at for months. His fingers were long and delicate, like a woman's. Seemed to me like they should have been playing a cello instead of cleaning an M-60.

"Nice to meet you, Jake." I didn't really feel that. I didn't feel anything as he smiled at me.

I switched my gaze to the Marine whom I vaguely knew and tried to cipher his name stamped on the front of his utility jacket. I raised my eyebrows. "When did you get this plush duty, Sims?"

"October. I heard they were looking for an armorer. I applied and got a transfer. Lucky for me, huh?"

I thought about that word, lucky. I nodded. "Yeah."

I stacked my weapon and magazines on the counter as I said, "I know a guy that got transferred to Division and now he's a courier and another guy who drives the division chaplain around. I wonder why I didn't luck out and get one of those billets."

Jake looked up from the M-60. "Maybe you're too valuable in the bush."

I laughed as I imagined myself crawling around in a trench, scared shitless, head down, trying to make it until my time in-country wound down. I smiled. "Yeah, maybe."

Sims pulled a five-by-eight file card out of a Marine Corps-green metal box. He said, "Let's see what you're supposed to turn in. The usual, I suppose. Standard issue."

He stood up and walked over to the counter. I noticed his brand new jungle boots. I looked down at mine and he picked up my M-16 and read the serial number silently as he made sure it was the correct one. His thin lips mouthed the digits. He handed it to Jake. "Needs cleaning."

He counted my magazines. "You're short seven."

"I know. I left them with the people who need them."

He nodded and then glared at me. "Got any other weapons?"

I pursed my lips and stared at him. He squinted back. I reached into the utility pocket on the right side of my trousers and pulled out a black K-bar knife. I smiled at him as I hefted it several times and then handed it to him.

He looked at my record and said, "Never issued to you."

I rolled my eyes and bit the end of my tongue. "I know that. Lots of weapons get passed around up there on the plateau. Some never been recorded to anybody. We took what we needed, especially after somebody bought the fucking farm."

He glared. "Why didn't you leave the damned thing up there? Now I have to fuck with all this gungy-green Marine Corps bullshit documentation."

"It makes me feel safe."

"What, Corporal Adams?"

"I might have to stab a gook."

They both laughed. Jake said, "You don't need to worry about that back here. We've got more protection around here than we need."

I thought about all those gooks out there in the rice paddies, the jungles, and how many Americans they had massacred outside the American Embassy in Saigon, at the old imperial capital at Hue, places that had more protection than they needed. I mumbled under my breath, "You should be so lucky."

Sims looked at his wristwatch. "Almost time to knock off. We need to finish up." He shook his head in short quick arcs and checked over my gear then looked at my file. "Hmm, short a lot of gear, Adams. And you have gear not issued to you. I don't know if I can overlook this. We may have to write you ... "

I yelled, "What the fuck, we're fighting a war."

Sims looked at me with his mouth open and Jake stifled a laugh. I felt my fists ball up, but Sims was in charge so I had to take my medicine.

He grinned. "Just fucking with you, man."

My gut burned and I wondered if I'd eaten too much gravy at chow. As I sneered at the two and turned to leave, Sims slapped the countertop and said, "Hold on, Adams, we were just kidding you. You need to sign some forms anyway."

I stopped and glared. The two men smiled. I signed the first form and said, "What's today's date?"

Sims smiled again, started to say something but then changed his mind. "Four April, Nineteen-sixty-eight."

I wrote the date on the form and noticed my full signature. I hadn't seen that for months. It looked strange to me, like I was reading someone else's name—a date that had no meaning to me.

Pissed off, but relieved, too, I signed and dated the other forms then slid them over to Sims and said, "Thanks."

I turned to leave as Sims said, "Where you headed now?"

"Back to the transient barracks."

He said, "Why don't we go get a beer?"

I stopped. "The club open?"

He looked at Jake and they both smiled. Jake said, "Club's not open till sixteen-hundred hours."

"I don't feel like waiting." I wanted to read Jinny's letter.

Sims said, "We can go right now—a different club."

I hesitated and he continued, "Come on man, I want to talk to you about some of the guys up there."

"I don't want to talk about 'up there.'"

He frowned and I said, "I need to go to Disbursing and get paid. I don't have any money."

He reached back like he was grabbing his wallet. "I'll buy."

I didn't want to go with them. I said, "Okay."

Sims clapped his hands and said, "Lance Corporal

Jacobs, secure the area. It's o-beer-thirty."

Jake stacked paperwork in neat little piles and I thought about all my Beatles albums stacked in a neat pile in Leanna's bedroom. Her frilly white bedcover with her frilly pillows and her white teddy bears. John Lennon's nasal voice came to mind. That's who I liked. I didn't like Paul and the rest of them very much. Only as much as they could help John sound good. I thought about Jinny and Leanna dancing around to the sound of "Norwegian Wood."

I tried to remember the lyrics. *I once had a ...* or was it, *I once loved a girl, or should I say, she once loved me.* That seemed wrong.

The thought of them dancing around with each other made me remember silly things the Beatles did in the movie *Hard Day's Night*, like running around wearing stupid clothes and acting like they didn't have a lick of sense. Jinny and Leanna would do something like that. Just for fun.

Sims waved at me to follow and we walked out of the back of the metal building. The red ground looked harsh. The sun had heated the surface and its reflection burned my face.

Sims and Jake walked over to a Mighty-Mite and got in and started the engine. I thought, how the hell you rate a Mighty-Mite?

Sims said, "Come on. Get in. It's beer time."

I got in and sat in the back and we pulled around a bunch of green metal buildings and down a street, up to a sandbagged gate with Marines manning fighting positions and machine gun pits. Behind that, on the side of the road, a Patton tank was dug in behind a red-earth berm with its 120-millimeter cannon pointed at the gate. Camouflage netting hung over the tank position and reminded me of lace doilies on Leanna's mother's coffee table.

Marines lounged around in green t-shirts playing cards. One sunned himself on a sandbag wall, his skinny chest exposed, and another took a nap. Pretty loose, I thought.

Luke-the-gook comes down that road, these turds will be in for a very unpleasant surprise. You pogues best tighten your asses up or you'll need more than luck to stay alive.

We drove through the gate and nobody even halted us. Sims nodded and yelled somebody's name, but I didn't catch it. Little black birds sat on top of a sign that said, "1st Battalion, 26th Marine Regiment."

Red dust flowed from behind the Mighty-Mite. The breeze in my hair felt weird and I missed my helmet. I started to reach for my rifle, but then I remembered. I put on my soft cover and pulled the bill down tight, but I still felt naked.

I glanced around the inside of the vehicle but only noticed one weapon, a dull black .45 caliber pistol. I yelled into Jake's ear, "That the only weapon we got?"

He looked at me and frowned. "What?"

I pointed at the .45 and said, "That all we got?"

He smiled and said, "Relax. You aren't up on that damned plateau now."

I sat back in my seat and sucked in a deep breath and held it for seven or eight seconds. I closed my eyes and stretched my neck back and tried to relax but all I could think about was gooks popping up on the red-tiled roofs of the buildings we passed. I folded my arms and opened my eyes and looked at all the black metal gates and the Vietnamese words written in bright red on the sides of whitewashed buildings. I noted the people as they stared at us. Their stony gazes confirmed my suspicions.

Sims honked the Mighty-Mite's horn and waved at everybody he saw—Marines and gooks—like they were all his best friends and there wasn't a war going on. I kept turning around in my seat, watching the men and women as we sped by. I didn't want one of them to shoot me in the back.

I put one leg underneath me on the seat so I could move around better and look in all directions.

Sims turned to me and smiled. "Relax, goddamnit.

We're safe."

A sudden urge to grab his shoulders came over me. I wanted to scream as I shook him, "This is piss-poor, raggedy-ass security, Sims. You want to die young?"

Instead, I crossed my arms and watched the road ahead as the sudden green of jungle closed in on us. Limbs of tall trees hung over the road and the underbrush was a thick, dark, jade-colored screen. My heart pounded as my chest started to burn. Sims and Jake were talking but I couldn't understand their words.

We passed rice paddies where old men stood knee-deep in water, hands full of long, thin, green plants. They wore big, flat, yellowed conical hats. They reminded me of long-legged water birds ... pond herons or cattle egrets.

On dikes separating the rice paddies, lime-colored plants with big fronds. I imagined myself lying in the red mud on the other side of one of those dikes, a scope on my rifle. I'd love to take a crack at blowing the top of Sims' head off, or Jake's. If I was a gook. I pulled my arms tighter around my chest as I thought, dumb fuckers, nobody wearing helmets or flak jackets.

I closed my eyes again and tried to dream about home. Who was I going to see first when I got there? Leanna? I'd call as soon as I got to LA. I thought about her and me dancing real close to "Norwegian Wood."

Again I tried to remember. *She told me she worked da-da-da-da and started to laugh. I told her I didn't da-da-da to sleep in the bath.*

I tried imagining me and my other friends, too, listening to Beatles albums—the new ones I knew must have come out—but images of Luke-the-gook popping out from behind the trunk of an ancient tree kept invading my head, jumbling with my friends. My neck felt like huge fingers pinched into the flesh around my spine, constricting the movement of my head and shoulders.

Suddenly the Mighty-Mite slowed. I opened my eyes as

we approached a small ville located on the left side of the road. Tall trees shaded what looked like a whole series of whitewashed old French style buildings with red tiles on the roofs. On the right sat rice paddies that looked like they reached all the way to the mountains along the Laotian border. Between the rice paddies and the ville was a three-roll concertina wire barrier backed by sandbagged fighting positions with slit trenches behind that. I shuddered as I thought about Luke coming across those flats in the misty night, in a steady monsoon drizzle.

Sims turned the vehicle down a shaded dirt street. Whitewashed houses with outbuildings stood on both sides of the road. We passed a small Catholic church with a small white cross on top. About three buildings down and across the street we stopped in front of an old building with rusty bars over the windows. A healthy grove of tall thin trees surrounded a reed-covered veranda.

I recognized the ville as one of those places where Marines lived right beside the locals and tried to keep Luke from coming in and taking over. A civic action platoon or something like that. I didn't like the look of it, the way it sat isolated, surrounded by rice paddies, miles from Phu Bai and no towers or strong defense system.

Out in the paddies people worked. I relaxed and thought, hell, they aren't going to attack this place while it's still light. I thought this even as I realized that all those men and women out there were probably Luke-the-gook as soon as the sun went down.

I grabbed Jake's shoulder and said, "What's the name of this place?"

Sims told me but it was all gook to me and besides I was already wondering what it would be like serving with a civic action platoon in this place. Ten or twelve Marines weren't going to stop Luke if he wanted to come inside.

Sims and Jake got out of the Mighty-Mite and Sims ordered, "Let's get our beer."

They walked over to an outdoor seating area under the reed-covered veranda. Cheap wooden chairs and tables were scattered randomly on a raised wooden deck. I followed them as I kept swiveling my head around, checking the perimeter. I searched for a place to hide, maybe a shed or a house. I sat in a chair with my back against a low, whitewashed wall.

A middle-aged gook broad came out of the building and smiled, "Hey, Sims. Hey, Jake. Wanna beer?"

Sims smiled and said, "You bet, Thuy."

She smiled at me. Her teeth were stained. She nodded. "How about your buddy?"

I said, "No."

Sims chuckled. "Yeah, three beers. Very cold, Mama-san, very cold."

She giggled and went inside a small, thatch-covered hooch and pulled up the top of one of those antique beer coolers that open like a chest.

Sims put his hand on my shoulder. "Relax, man. These are good people. There isn't any ground-up glass in the drinks they serve."

I stared at the table top.

Mama-san brought out three beers. I watched Sims and Jake take big swallows. Their Adam's apples moved up and down. I grabbed the long, dark brown glass neck of my beer bottle. The label was orange with black gook writing on it. Lots of A's with upside-down scimitars over them, and chevrons too, and chevrons over the E's and O's. Nothing I could cipher.

Sims smirked at me and shook his head.

Jake and he started talking to each other about working in the armory and about how much more time each one had left in-country and where Jake wanted to go on R & R. Sims swallowed a mouthful of beer and said, "Bangkok."

I took a sip of my beer. I didn't like the taste of it. Too thick and bitter.

Jake said, "Why not Sydney or Hawaii?"

I thought about cans of cold Coors in a five-gallon bucket, on ice. The lighter taste, the lighter color.

Sims said, "Cheaper pieces of ass. Besides, do you want to spend your whole life just fucking white girls?"

Jake's face turned red as he laughed. "I haven't ever fucked anybody."

Sims slapped him on the shoulder and said, "Congratulations for being man enough to admit that."

I imagined the bucket of beer on top of the trunk to my old man's car. Parked beside a cotton field in the steamy night. Leanna and me in the back seat. Her flat. Me on top. I tried to recall the words to the song. *We da* ... my inability to remember the lyrics pissed me off ... *until two, and then she said, da-da-da-da.*

A transistor radio on top of the car. The sound of crickets and frogs peeping in the moonlit night. I reached in my pocket and got the letter from Jinny.

As I started to open the letter two young Marines walked down the road. They wore combat gear and had rifles slung in reverse over their shoulders, the muzzles pointed at the ground. I could tell by the cut of their jaws and cheeks they hadn't seen much combat. Too fat. I wondered if they were former pogues. Re-upped for the cash bonus. Sims yelled, "Tom, what's to it? You too, Jim?"

Tom said, "Nothing to it."

Mama-san brought beers for them as they sat chatting with Jake and Sims.

Across the red dirt street in somebody's garden two very tall birds with red and green heads sat watching us. They had long, elegant necks. I turned Jinny's letter over once or twice.

Again, the search for the correct words. *She told me she worked in da-da-da and hmm-hmm-hmm-hmmmm. I da-da I didn't and da-da-da-da-da the bath.*

I looked at the birds again and watched as they slowly

hunted on long stilt-like legs. I wondered when Luke would decide to hit this place. Some rainy night when our air power wasn't effective. They'd Bangalore the wire and come through, their brassy horns blaring, the shriek of their metal whistles and their screams raising the hair on the back of these two Marines' necks. They'd come in with mortar fire and RPGs and AKs chattering up the night, needle bayonets out, looking for a torso to stab. And the mama-san serving us beers would shoot Tom and Jim in the back. That is if they were lucky. And if they didn't get killed in the initial assault? Who knows? Hung up and skinned like pigs in a slaughterhouse—a long slow death. Their balls sliced off and sewed up in their mouths.

My inability to get the song right irritated me. *And when I awoke, da-da-da-da, this bird had flown.*

I closed my eyes and heard flies buzzing. One of those large red-and-green-headed birds let out a sound like, "Skrake, skrake." One of the Marines was talking about the Phillies and the Cubs and somebody said something about his girl. I opened my eyes and opened the letter.

Jinny's neat little scrawl was etched on the pages. "I think I'm going to get straight A's for the third straight semester, so that I should graduate in the top five-percent of my class.

"Alois Murphy was killed in Saigon in the Tet Offensive. My dad read it in the paper last week. He wondered why it took 'so damned long' (as he put it) for us to find out.

"Lanny Jones and Trisha Stevens got married on the QT. No guests at the wedding, just the justice of the peace, the parents and Trisha's little brother. I wonder what happened. Ha-ha."

Not a word about Leanna. I finished reading the letter and shut my eyes as I thought about her closing sentence.

I heard the very tall birds with the red and green heads flap their long wings and "skrake" in harsh tones. In the fields the sound of the gooks talking their outer-space lingo floated towards me and mixed with the mama-sans' jabbering around the ville. Somewhere a baby squalled and children clapped their hands and sang songs in Vietnamese, or was it French? The tension would not retreat from my neck. I heard a water buffalo bellow over the grab-assing of Jake and Sims and the other two. A breeze whispered over the top of the veranda as my beer got warm.

"You're not going to like what's happened to your Beatles albums. Love, Jinn."

Cinco de Mayo

It was Cinco de Mayo, my last day on leave. The next day I had to fly back to Camp Pendleton to play Marine and play war games and wait to maybe go across the Pacific pond to Vietnam and a second tour of fighting. I got up early and drove to Tucson. I arrived before they expected and interrupted them in bed, my old school chum and his girlfriend named Kate who I'd actually known longer than him. They acted like it was a sin getting caught *inflagrante delicto*. That made me laugh—as if I gave a damn.

I wouldn't let them get dressed in privacy. I wouldn't allow them to maintain any sort of propriety. Kate's apartment wasn't made for privacy anyway, with one large, open room and a head with a crapper and a shower. Lots of tall windows lit up the big room looking north to the still-winter-up-there snow-capped peak of Mt. Lemmon. I slouched at her yellow-topped kitchen table, waiting as they struggled to cover themselves with the tangled sheets. From the way my friend glared at me, I could tell I was in for one of his regular chastisings. Before he could start his rant, Kate got out of bed. As she took her first step, a corner of her sheet caught beneath her foot and exposed her bare legs, chest and ass.

He said, "Get back in here and I'll give you your ... ," but she reached down, put her hand over his mouth and said, "Shush."

I cracked up laughing, but stopped when he sneered at

me. She stumbled for a moment and I got a pretty good look—she didn't have much up top, but I also got a quick glimpse of her naked calves and thighs, nice and muscled. As a bonus she showed me her patch of pubic hair. I wondered if that was on purpose, but then I figured maybe not, because her face was as red as Rocco's 1968 Ford Mustang outside the window. I hid my chuckle as I remembered her in fourth grade, so serious. A smart, pretty gal.

I smoked a quarter of a pack of Camels before they both dressed. They ate poached eggs and wrangled about them with their mouths full—he didn't think they were cooked enough.

I declined breakfast and smoked another Camel and drank black coffee.

He looked up at me while he used toast to sop up egg. "Why don't you go get Denise?"

"Who's that?"

"Your date."

"I don't know where she lives."

He frowned. "I'll give you directions."

I flicked Camel ashes into a saucer on the table. "I don't need a date."

Kate's eyes got big and she looked at me like I was nuts. "The last twenty days you've been doing nothing but pining about getting laid."

"I didn't say that."

"You didn't have to."

Rocco got up and glared. "You won't go get her?"

"It was your idea—you want her to come, then you go get her."

He slapped the palm of his hand on the table. "Okay, forget it then."

Kate grabbed his right arm. "We can't do that." She smirked at him. "I thought this was all set up."

He wouldn't look at her. "I didn't think we'd have to go through this—I thought he'd want to have a nice honey to go with."

I didn't like the way they talked about me without looking at me. "I don't need any damned honey."

He barked, "What is wrong with you?"

I stood and put the palms of my hands on the table, not slapping them hard like he did, and leaned over so I was close to Rocco's face, "I don't give a fuck about ..."

Kate hugged him close and said to me, "It doesn't matter. We understand." She smiled and went on, "But it's too late to break the date." Her eyes were a funny color of blue and then I remembered she wore contact lenses and they must be tinted. She went on, "Can you agree to be civil?" She raised her eyebrows as if that might be a problem for me.

I grabbed the pack of Camels out of my pocket and fished a smoke and lit it up. "Yeah."

Kate smiled at me and said, "We'll go get her."

As they left to get the blind date, my old school chum stalked up and asked, "What in the fuck is the matter with you?"

I looked past him at the craggy heights of Mt. Lemmon through the tall windows. "Nothing."

While they picked her up, I inhaled a third of a pack of Camels and swilled the pot of coffee they left on the stove. I tried to read the newspaper but all it had was stories about the killing in Nam and worse than that, all the war protests. I found a can of Sunday morning Coors hidden behind the milk in the refrigerator. I killed it in big swallows before they could come back and catch me drinking. I thought about the blind date. I knew her from grade school.

I thought about the hookers in Bangkok. How they tried to steal money out of my wallet after I got done coming. How they giggled when the Air Force lifers took their children and vacated the Post Exchange bowling alley when we showed up to knock some pins down. And downtown

near the geedunk shops they'd grab onto you and beg you
to buy them gold pendants on heavy gold chains, and gray-
colored star sapphires and leather mini-skirts.

I heard the engine rumble on the red Mustang and it
didn't take long before the horn honked. So I stopped day-
dreaming about whores and how pissed off one of them
would get if she thought another whore was getting more
of my money. I walked downstairs and up to the car as
the day shone a happy green of elm trees and palo verdes
and the songs of warblers. I got in the car and sat in the
cramped back seat next to my blind date while we drove
the ninety miles to Nogales, Mexico. I'd known her back
in the fourth grade. Me and her and Kate went way back
when we all lived in the little cotton-farming town where
we grew up northwest of Tucson.

What the fuck was I doing, living in the past, the fourth
grade? She'd changed—grew up slim and angular, owned
a hooked nose—more than hooked—a hatchet face. I
remembered her as cute, with a pageboy haircut and a big
smile. She still had short bangs and her hair cut up under
her ears and a big smile, but her teeth were way too big
now, and her elbows looked like knots on the roots of elm
trees. Out of the corner of my eye I could see her looking at
me. I didn't like that … what the hell was there about me to
be figured out?

When we first got in the car she hugged me—kind of like
a long lost friend would do. I couldn't respond. In the back
seat of that red 1968 Mustang, she sat close to me and
once she tried to take my hand.

The last time I'd been in Nogales there was no four-lane,
and the town was ramshackle red and blue stucco and
pink and yellow with brightly painted wooden lintels and
window frames, and a lot of dogs running loose along the
streets. The dogs were still there.

I said to my date, "If I had my rifle I'd kill all those dogs."

Rocco said, "This isn't the sheep fields, *mi amigo*, those are someone's pets."

I said, "I choose to recall what my father had to say about dogs."

Kate giggled, "What comments did your father make— I'd like to know what he thought about dogs."

"One dog's not too bad, two dogs are half a dog and three dogs are no dog at all."

Rocco and Kate laughed knowingly and I couldn't cipher if it was because they knew dogs or they knew my father. My date put her large, long-fingered hand over her big teeth and giggled.

Kate said, "I haven't seen your father for a long time."

They all knew him back in the day, except for Rocco who knew him well enough now. He'd been a PE teacher. He'd treated all of us like we were a pack of dogs he could order around, and if we didn't obey, he'd whip us with a paddle.

I said, "He's doing what he always does."

I watched a large black Great Dane trotting towards us as if he owned the road. His head must have been close to five feet above the pavement. He moved his head back and forth as if he were surveying a kingdom and his jowls hung down and jiggled with every step he took.

I said, "Goddamnit, I wish I had my M-16 right now."

Rocco said, "I don't carry firearms anymore. Something only good for destruction, tools of the military industrial complex."

I thought about my past thirteen months and what would have happened to me if I hadn't carried a firearm— those millions of gooks that wanted to shoot me dead. What the hell did these people in their brand-spanking-new 1968 red Mustang produced by the military industrial complex think the world was like? Even though they didn't look it, they reminded me of hippie-types so I let my violent talk subside. I didn't want to "bring them down" as the current saying went. I doubted if they had a clue about lighting gooks' asses up—it wasn't "cool."

At the border between Nogales, Arizona, and Nogales, Mexico, the line of autos crept. It amazed me that that many Americans would be interested in a Cinco de Mayo celebration. They must have agreed with Rocco—when he invited me to come along he said the celebration would be groovy, whatever that means. Most of the people going south were gringos like us driving big Dodges and Buicks and Lincoln Continentals. When we got into Mexico the cramped streets teemed with *turistas* wearing big straw sombreros and cheap wool serapes. From the car, I saw an old gringo lady shaking some varnished wood maracas. Her husband wore castanets on his fingers and he clicked them as he sashayed around her in a continuous clockwise motion. They walked down the street liked they owned it, playing their new-bought instruments.

I mumbled, "Damned fools."

Kate looked at me with dark eyes that scolded. "They are just trying to have some fun."

Old hatchet-nose let out a knowing laugh and tried to take my hand again.

Rocco looked at me in his rear-view mirror. His dark eyes and curly brown hair made his red face stand out. I could tell by the way his eyes bored into me he wasn't happy.

In the big dirt parking lot outside the bullring he turned and leaned towards me, "What the hell's the matter with you?"

I was thinking I'd say "None of your fucking business," but instead I just shook my head twice and said, "Nothing."

He got out and walked around the car and opened Kate's door and grabbed her hand and said, "Let's go."

As he dragged her off by the left arm she looked back at me and raised her eyebrows, smiled and shrugged.

I got out of the car and fired up a Camel, leaned against

the red fender while I waited for the blind date to get out so we could go inside and watch somebody butcher bulls.

We waited in a line with a lot of local Mexican men wearing grey and tan suits and fancy fedoras. The white-washed walls reflected heat. I couldn't understand a damn thing any of those Mexicans were saying. In big black and red lettering, the posters on the walls announced a list of matadors. Those colors reminded me of the whores in Bangkok. I glanced at Kate and the blind date. Somehow they seemed like babies compared to the whores. At the Bangkok bowling alley I had put my hands flat on the plastic chairs on either side of me as I sat down. They both giggled and sat on my hands. They weren't wearing under-wear. We had a great laugh at the expense of the Air Force lifers' wives.

I looked at Kate again. There was something about her profile that made me need to stand on one leg, then the other.

While we waited, Rocco gave me the scuttlebutt on the rules of bullfighting. Men ride horses into the ring and stab the bull in the shoulders with long spears. The bulls try to gore the horses, but the *caballos* wear protective armor that looks like quilts draped on their bodies so there's no way they can get hurt, or so the thinking goes. The crowd cheers.

Inside, sitting high above the sandy bullring bottom, I took my first pull on a long-necked bottle of Modeno. The warmth of it jolted me and reminded me of a story my father told me about going into a bar in Australia in World War II. Three Marines came in and ordered beer and when they found out it wasn't ice cold, spit it out and said it tasted like piss. My father said some Aussie soldiers then proceeded to kick the Marines' asses. I hated that, having him tell me, having to listen to him tell me. And he'd make sure he told me. He hated Marines, or so I'd heard him say all my life. And then I up and joined the Marines.

Ken Rodgers

The matadors stabbed the *toros* with little *banderillas*
that stayed in the muscles and jerked around like child's
toys when the bull charged—and he charged. Reminded
me of how men get ferocious when cornered.

The second day home from the war I told my father
about a ridge we assaulted just below the DMZ the day
before I left Nam. The first two platoons of Marines that hit
the ridge caught the gooks not paying attention and gave
them a serious fucking-up. But there were a lot more gooks
up there than we thought and they eventually mauled our
boys pretty bad and then it was my turn to face AK-47s
and RPGs and 60MM mortars and machine gun gristle.
We went in there and shot the shit out of the rest of those
gooks and ran their asses off that ridge. Near the top I
stumbled into a bomb crater and found three Marines lying
there, still breathing and still grinning, with eyes glazed
over, remnants of absolute fear. There were lots of dead
gooks piled in there too. Black flies swarmed in a black
cloud over the crater and battled over pools of drying
blood. I smelled human shit.

When I told my father that story he looked straight
ahead, never looked at me and never acted like he heard
a word of it. I bet that galled his butt, tough guy that he
thought he was—spent all his time in World War II pumping airplane fuel into cargo planes in India. Never even
fired his rifle in anger or in combat. I got some payback for
him fucking with me all my life.

After all the stabbing and poking, the bulls charged the
horses, trying to puncture muscle with thick, wide horns.
Then the matadors brought out their red capes. The bull
and the matador did their deadly dance. This happened
one bull at a time, all the stabbing, the *picadoring*, the
deadly dancing. The first two matadors couldn't kill their
bulls; they kept stabbing and stabbing. Finally they had to
sever the bulls' spinal cords with a tool that was more like
a machete than the customary sword. The matadors didn't

get the ears or anything, and the crowd wasn't cheering. The dead bulls were the real heroes.

It was hot and I didn't finish my beer. It made me gag. Hatchet-nose cheered. So did Rocco and Kate. The last matador was the big name on the marquee and I quickly understood why. He had panache and his dance showed the most heart. He stabbed the bull, right in the heart on the first attempt, right through a tiny triangle of soft tissue nested between the muscles where the bull's back and neck met, straight into the heart. The crowd cheered and threw fedoras—some women threw bouquets of red roses. Red petals flew off the stems when the bouquets hit the ground. The deep red color seemed to light up against the tan of the dirt. I looked at the concrete deck beneath my feet and the glare from the whitewashed stucco walls burned my head. It was starting to spin along with my stomach.

The matador got the ears—he held them up to the cheering crowd, reminding me of the gladiator movies my old man used to take me to when I was a kid, the victorious gladiator—yeah, the ears and maybe some other parts of the bull, I couldn't watch—and some amount of money I am sure. The sun loomed overhead and I felt my underarms dripping with sweat.

Rocco jammed the thumb and middle finger of his right hand between his lips and let out a whistle so sharp I thought he'd pounded nails into my eardrums. Kate jumped up and down and then hopped over in front of me, clutching my shoulders. She shook me and screamed, "*Muy bien, muy bien*." My blind date kept trying to hold my hand. I tried to drink my beer again but it tasted like warm urine.

I flipped a Camel out of my cigarette package and lit it with my silver lighter, the one with the map of Vietnam on it, but the smoke burned my throat and the inside of my mouth tasted like ashes so I tossed the cigarette on the deck and ground it out with my boot heel. Then I rose. I had to escape, staggered down the aisle, bumping into elated, screaming patrons. An elbow from an excited fanatic hit me just above the eye and the sensations radiated through the hard bone into the middle of my head. I pushed him saying, "Get the fuck out of the way."

He reached to grab my arm as I got out on the stairway that led to the exit, but I slapped at him as I started to trot up the stairs. I heard him yelling, "*Pinche gringo. Pinche cabrón.*"

At the exit, I turned around and looked at the ring as workmen in big straw sombreros dragged the bull away with a trace of horses. One of the dead bull's horns gouged the dirt and left a deep furrow that filled with a mixture of mud and blood that accentuated the brilliance of the rose petals.

I suddenly saw those three Marines in that bomb crater up at the DMZ, saw their smiling blood-stained faces, their ripped biceps and a leg with a web belt for a tourniquet missing everything below the knee.

I rushed out of the bullring and found a place in the shade. Heat waffled off the parking lot. I watched the waves simmer skyward as I leaned against the wall, my hands behind me with palms flat against the stucco to steady me against its subtle curve. The wall felt cool and helped me as I tried to force the gorging nausea to go away.

Rocco walked up with the women. He looked at me like a vulture, as if hovering, ready to attack, but Kate smiled at me and said, "You all right?"

I nodded and thought about her back in high school, how all us boys used to walk home after football practice and talk about her. We'd say, "Man, I'd like to *get* her."

My blind date stood next to me as if to offer something to steady myself on. I didn't accept. Rocco said to no one in particular, "Great finish, huh?"

Kate shrugged and turned one side of her mouth up. My blind date stared at me. I could feel her concern on the side of my face. I turned to look at her and noticed the color and texture of her irises. Reminded me of marbles we used to play with in the dirt at South School. The centers were vibrant swirls of color frozen in the glass of the taws. Hers, in this light, were a brilliant violet that I couldn't stand to look at for more than two or three seconds. I slumped down the wall and sat on the ground.

Rocco looked down at me. "I liked the way the last matador killed the bull."

"He was good," my blind date said, "but the others were worthless."

Then Rocco added, "Goes with the territory."

Kate frowned, "What does that mean, territory?"

He told her, "That's just bullfighting."

I looked up at him and said, "That's butchery and murder."

He laughed at me. "Aren't we being a little hypocritical?"

I looked at the ground.

My blind date chimed in, "What does that mean, hypocritical, in this context?"

He didn't stop staring down at me, "He knows what Marines do. They participate in butchery."

I sensed both of the women looking at me. He knelt down and peered into my face. I could see blackheads on his nose. He asked, "Isn't that right, old friend?"

I said, "Exactly."

We went downtown and walked around the plaza and my old school chum made reservations to eat at La Cueva. He said, "That's the best place to eat down here." He used his big index finger to poke me in the chest as we walked along, and went on expounding, "Used to be the jail. Imagine that, cramming a bunch of pickpockets and thieves in a cave in the side of a hill. No ventilation in summer, no heat in winter."

I wondered what he thought they ought to do that would work any better with thieves than treating them like the vermin they were.

As we came around a corner, we saw Indians performing some kind of ceremony in a large plaza. They intertwined themselves with thick ropes. This all took place at the top of a pole at least a hundred feet tall. They wore fancy head-dresses that looked like small palm trees. The ropes were tied to their legs and I suspected that they were all going to get themselves in some kind of knot and then somehow resolve the situation for our entertainment. One, who didn't have a rope, sat on top of the pole, although I didn't know how he could do that without losing his balance and falling off.

We stopped on the sidewalk, big gringo Lincolns and Chevys parked against the curb on one side, the plaza on the other.

Rocco demanded, "Did you hear what I said?"

"What?"

He barked. "You should pay more attention. I said, 'No heat in winter, no ventilation in summer. La Cueva.'"

I said, "Right. Brutal."

I heard yelling. Apparently we were to meet up with some of their college law school friends. They hollered us down and there was a lot of jive-assing around—these new people needed haircuts, their clothes were unkempt, pin-striped bellbottoms and loose, flowery, womanish shirts. Two were in law school with Rocco. They all smelled of hard liquor and screamed about some politician named Eugene McCarthy who might just be the next president and would end the war.

I wondered who Eugene McCarthy was. I lit a Camel and savored the way it made my lungs silently whine for more. Rocco and the newcomers rattled on among themselves about politics and I watched the Indians on the pole.

One of the law students kept yelling, "Clean Gene."

In the plaza I noticed an elderly woman in a long dress walking a small dog—a miniature poodle or something like that. My comrades laughed at the loud-mouthed law student as he jumped on the hood of a nearby car and yelled "Clean Gene, Clean Gene."

I yelled, "Knock it off before somebody shoots your stupid fucking ass."

He glared and yelled back, "It's only Mexico."

The old woman's small poodle lifted its leg and peed on a trash can full of paper plates and empty, brown Corona and Tres Equis bottles.

My father liked to say, "I have the solution for Mexico. Send in the Army, throw out all those old, rich families and give them an ultimatum: English-based law, or forever be our province." He would double up his fist when he said that and bend his arm and make a muscle and slap it and smile. The thought of him and his silly muscle and his sillier ultimatum made me smile and think of Vietnam and how he'd have hacked all that chaos.

But I didn't smile at the loudmouth lawyer jumping up and down on the car, drawing a crowd of locals saying a lot of stuff in Mexican I didn't understand. Some of the stuff sounded curious, and from the looks on those faces, some words a little more hostile.

I walked thirty or forty yards away as if I didn't know my party and watched the Indians. A few minutes later Kate came over and when I looked at her she raised her eyebrows and gave a little shrug.

Then, four of the Indians with the ropes tied to their legs let go of the skyscraper-high pole they clung to and the pole began to turn just the littlest bit and they began to unravel themselves and the Indian on top stood up on one leg and began to play a flute. He looked like some kind of Aztec god up there, Huitzilopoctli or Quetzacoatal. I wondered how he kept from dying of fright or from losing confidence and falling the long distance to the concrete paving the plaza.

I could hear Rocco and the blind date and the would-be lawyers prattling on over by the cars about this Eugene

McCarthy and Lyndon Baines Johnson and Bobby Kennedy and how Kennedy had to become the next president so the war would really end. The McCarthy advocate tried to talk louder than everyone else but Rocco was still the loudest.

The pole went around faster and faster the farther the Indians flew away from the center, centrifugal motion giving the thing speed.

I hunched my shoulders and looked at the cracks in the concrete and the grass punching through and dragged the front sole of my boot on the cement. I chuckled about Kennedy and Johnson and how nobody would stop the war until the motion that drove it ran out of steam. People weren't in charge, they could only react.

When I looked up at the pole, all the Indians were on the ground except the one who had been at the top, and he was on his way down.

The sound of guitars and coronets and violins waffled on the afternoon breeze. Kate looked up and smiled and signaled to some mariachis that strolled along the sidewalk playing Mexican music. They stopped playing and walked toward us and Kate tried to give them some money, but I grabbed her hand and nodded at them and dug my wallet out of my back pocket and said, "La Cucaracha." She offered me a grin that glinted brightly compared to all the carnival hoopla going on in the plaza.

The mariachis were dressed in what I figured must have been traditional costume. The color of their uniforms was a tepid forest green with blood-red piping on the jackets and the trousers. Their red high-heeled riding boots were scuffed, with silver tips on the pointed toes. They wore white shirts stained with sweat and dust and large, heavy sombreros shaded their heads.

One hombre, who must have been the *jefe*, carried a dented silver-colored coronet and one had a fiddle, and there were several guitars, including a guitarron with a backside that reminded me of one-half of a giant gourd.

The coronet rang and the big guitarron thumped into spontaneous music and the melody lilted across the Bermuda grass that choked the privet bushes and the pyracantha. The fiddle came in behind with a refrain that reminded me of a Marine who got too far behind a patrol looking for a firefight.

Watching Kate watch them and smile, I decided to buy a number of other songs, and asked her what she wanted to hear and she said "Almahada" which meant nothing to me, and she swayed instantly with the start of the music.

In the plaza I heard the yapping of a dog over the song and looked; the old lady's poodle had her leash pulled tight and was barking at a pack of black and white and brown mongrels that circled. I could see them baring their fangs and suddenly a dogfight broke out with a lot of dust and people kicking and screaming in Spanish. But that sound was drowned out by a fierce cheer and I noticed the Indians climbing back up that tall pole and I guess they'd be trying to unwind the troubles of the world again. In front of me and Kate, the mariachis thumped out "Besame Mucho." They smiled knowingly at Kate and me, as if they knew we were lovers.

The politics behind us got raucous but I refused to turn and watch because I know where politics gets you and my not-so-blind date giggled a lot, a giggle I was starting to not like, and then the would-be lawyers were suddenly gone.

Rocco hollered, "Time to eat," and we walked across a street filled with empty beer cans and cars honking and pushing along in a slow traffic jam. More than one group of mariachis sang and the sun hit the hills on the east side of town and lit up the saguaro cactus that stood up there.

We walked up to a set of double doors set into the side of a rock ledge. The wood of the doors was intricately carved with curlicues and flourishes.

Hanging above the doors a small sign said, La Cueva. Rocco held the door for us. Once inside he barged to the front of a crowded foyer and started talking to some important-looking guy in loud Spanish and before anybody who had been patiently waiting got a table, we were seated in a black leather booth in a small, dark alcove hacked from the solid rock of the hill. An amber-colored glass globe with a lighted candle inside gave off a faint glow capturing the bottom of my companions' faces, making them eerie, especially Rocco, who looked like some kind of devil when he smiled—his canines out of line with his bicuspids. Kate looked pretty good in the light, kind of flattered her high cheekbones and black hair. My blind date giggled and held her long fingers over her mouth like a conspirator.

By the time I dug a Camel out of the package in my pocket, Rocco had ordered me a margarita and lamb chops.

I said, "I don't want tequila. When it goes down it gets half way there and then wants to come back up."

Rocco said, "This is the good shit, not that crap you Marines drink on liberty."

"Just give me a beer and I don't want anything to eat."

I felt Kate's leg touch mine beneath the table and I wondered if she was trying to tell me something about not responding to Rocco or if it was some other message or no message at all.

He said, "You need to eat—it'll make you feel better."

The reflection of a red neon Cerveza sign over the bar gave a dim light. I was back in a cold January night in the mountains just below the DMZ. The dim, blinking lights of our gunships cut through the night-time mist. Long, wavy sprays of crimson tracers sliced through the black sky and I hoped burned up the gooks who lay hidden out there waiting to kill me.

The rest of my party talked about the best kind of lamb and I thought I don't like any of it, too bitter, the fat too gamey, too wild tasting—the taste of fear before slaughter, like maybe those bulls felt when they ran into the ring this morning and all that alien shouting from Mexican maniacs and Americans, too, begging for the scent. I knew that scent—smelled it on myself often.

The walls of the restaurant curved up towards a domed ceiling and all the sounds that people adjacent to the walls made—coughs, chairs scraping on the polished red concrete floor, whispers, the clang of silverware on plates, hisses—came up and swooped under the domed top and down other sides, far away from the source.

I wondered if my father had smelled that smell—of fear. He seemed to like to talk about kicking people's asses all the time. Maybe that's what he craved, that scent.

Someone in the restaurant was talking about the bulls from the morning. I could hear their words creeping down the walls. I heard a whispered, "I love you." And my old man always kicking dogs, shooting at cats, grabbing other men by the front of their shirts. He'd have loved the bullfight—would have admired the gore of it all.

I heard mumbling coming into our alcove but couldn't make out a word of it. My father would have laughed at me at that bullfight when I had to leave and go out and lean against the arena wall. He'd have laughed and told everybody to go look at me. He'd have said that to people he didn't even know, people who couldn't even speak English. He'd have clutched their shoulders and slapped their backs in celebration of discovering how weak I was.

Hisses slipped into the sound of my ken and somewhere someone said, "Motherfucker," and there was a woman's groan, as if she'd lost her daughter in a car wreck to a broken neck, a severed spine, and my father outside the bullring right next to Rocco, on his knees looking into my face saying, "What's the matter, toughie? Marine Corps make you a fucking pussy?"

My blind date sidled into my space and I couldn't get any farther away. I was against the cool wall and I suddenly had visions of men crammed inside here with pig-slop dinners and bad water, bull blood mixed with arena sand making mud and the hisses and whispers of the patrons and my father, so I got up and went to the bar using the excuse that I couldn't stand the notion of that damned sweet margarita and needed a *cerveza*.

But I didn't go to the bar. Instead I walked past the three-deep crowd in front of the bar and went outside and turned left up a street running parallel to a saguaro cacti-studded hill. I wandered in the dying light into a narrow street that went from pavement to oiled dust in about a hundred feet. Soon the street was full of whores and gringos negotiating to get laid. The whores wore mini-skirts that showed a lot of leg—red skirts, yellow skirts, loud colors that advertised. The gringos acted sneaky like they didn't want to get caught. The whores sidled close, rubbing short, bowed legs against Levis and brown summer slacks.

I heard mariachi music coming through the open doors of a *cantina* so I went inside to listen but it was only an old jukebox. I decided to have a beer to soothe my disappointment. "One Corona, cold please." I pointed to a Corona sign.

The *cantinero* slammed a sweating bottle of beer on the bar and said, "*Poco* chilly, *señor.*" He owned a big handle-bar mustache and the light caught the silver fillings in his teeth when he smiled.

There were four or five scoundrels drinking in there with me, all of us in solitary moods, no talking. My back felt cold and naked so I turned around and watched the others, my eyes flitting from one to another.

The needle on the arm of the record player in the neon red and blue jukebox caught in a worn-out music groove in the record's vinyl and played over and over and over, "*Te amo, Te amo, Te amo.*"

Nobody moved to fix it, just stared at each other, heads turning here and there like expectant hawks waiting for something to come out of a hole so they could kill it.

Before I knew it I'd drained five or six beers ... I lost count ... and as I was finishing the last one which had gotten quite warm, I noticed the hombre next to me whip out his pecker and piss in a trench in the floor that ran parallel to the bar, and I laughed out loud because I'd just been speculating on what the trench was for.

When I laughed, everybody snuck their beady eyes on me and I began to sweat as the jukebox cried, "*Te amo, Te amo*," and I suddenly felt as if hands were on my throat choking me like my father did once when I was seventeen and came home late from practicing my part in Shakespeare's *Hamlet*. Somebody walked over and with his knee drawn up high against his chest, kicked the jukebox and then smashed boot-bottom first against the glass again and again, but instead of resuming the love song, the thing just died and I ran outside and dropped on my knees next to the gutter in the street and puked my guts out—bad beer, hot beer, and something else I recognized but chose not to put a name to. It came up hot and scalded my throat and the inside of my nose. As I heaved, my ribs jammed up against my collarbone and my lungs felt like someone was standing on them.

I heard the hookers laughing and fully expected to be bonked on the head from behind and either robbed or killed, but neither happened. I stood and staggered away, heard snarls behind me and turned to see a pack of curs licking up my vomit. The meaner ones snapped at the weaker ones and a fight ensued. A whore in a red dress tried to break up the fight but a larger dog, part German shepherd, bit her hand. Somebody laughed and a mariachi standing outside another cantina picked up his coronet and blew one of those fanfares you hear before a horse race. Several hombres wearing huge, floppy straw sombreros started barking at each other in Spanish. I wondered if they were wagering on which dog would win.

My father kept trying his goddamnedest to get in my head, as did that big morning bull with the banderillas stuck in his bloody back. But I told them to get the fuck out. On a nearby corner, beneath a street lamp, I noticed a street vendor with one of those refrigerated ice cream boxes they push around on bicycle wheels. I bought an orange soda from him and paid in dollars which he smiled at because he preferred my money to his country's. I swished the strong, sweet liquid in my mouth then spit it out in a stream that landed on the oil-soaked street.

Back at La Cueva my lamb chops were cold and my margarita sat where the waiter left it, the tequila separated from the Cointreau like oil and water. Everybody was engrossed in conversation and Rocco didn't seem to have missed me, although my blind date grabbed my hand and squeezed it when I sat down, and Kate gave me one of those "and what have you been up to?" looks. When I shook my hand loose, my blind date let it go real quick. My skin retained a sense of her touch.

The women excused themselves and went to the head, and after frowning at me, Rocco did the same. I went outside and found a doorway to a saddle-maker's shop and leaned against the door out of the light. Pretty soon Kate came out and looked both ways and I stepped out into the light and when she saw me she smiled. I went back to being incognito and she came and stood beside me.

I suddenly had an urge to say something to her but words refused to come. She leaned into me. She felt warm and her soft hips fit nicely against mine. I grabbed her hand and she squeezed tight. I reached up and put my arm around her and pulled her close and gently kissed her and suddenly our tongues wrapped around each other. She jammed herself against my pelvis. I heard a loud cough and looked over her shoulder and saw Rocco walking down the sidewalk in the other direction. I squeezed the cheeks of Kate's ass and pushed her away.

I yelled at Rocco, "Down here."

On the way home, nobody talked. Kate fell asleep with her head on the door where the window should have been, but the night was pleasant and she had rolled it down. She snored a little and my blind date looked out her window at a full moon that was changing from something huge and round to something a little less overwhelming. She hummed a song with what I thought were the words, "The moon in Taurus," but I wasn't sure although I knew Taurus was a constellation that represented a bull but I didn't know where it stood in the wide-open night sky.

I tried to nap, but the noises of the day—the horns and castanets, the hookers making deals in Spanish, those Indians on that pole, and Gene McCarthy—kept jolting me awake just as my chin would hit my chest.

Once Rocco turned on the radio to some hippie underground station that played music with a refrain that kept banging through my head, but Kate came to and barked and when he tried to argue, she barked real loud. I had to stifle a laugh.

When we got back to Tucson I somehow got stuck taking the blind date home to her grandmother's house where she lived while attending the university. I wanted to send Rocco with her, but he shut me off before any opportunities for me and Kate came up. "Call us the next time you're on leave."

The night had turned soft and balmy and we rolled the windows down and the blind date gave me soft directions to head north and west. Ocotillo and cholla, ironwood trees studded the landscape. Scads of cottontail rabbits and once a sleek yellow coyote crossed the road in front of our headlights. She slid next to me and laid her head on my shoulder. I wanted to shake her off and she must have known it because she said, "I won't bite."

Somehow that made me think of the matadors who were trying to kill those bulls and how much guts it took to not bail out when the horns got near the abdomen. It made me think, too, about that Indian looking like Huitzilopoctli or some other Aztec god on top of that spinning pole that went faster and faster. I wanted to tell my father about seeing that—I bet he'd never seen anything like it. I wanted to ask him if he thought he had the guts to do that. And the thoughts of Kate, her scent, and her tongue.

I was still spinning with Kate and the Aztec when we got to my blind date's house and I felt honor-bound to walk her to the door. The night was bright and the scent of lavender came from somewhere in a large garden. There wasn't a light on in the house but I could tell it was surrounded by a screened-in porch—good for sleeping on hot summer nights. She grabbed my hand just as I was about to thank her and tell her how much fun we'd had and all that shit. She pulled me in through the porch and through a large door that was rounded on top and into a pitch-black room where the air was stiff and unwelcome.

I said, "Where's your grandma?"

She said, "Don't worry, she won't hear us."

I wondered what she meant by anybody hearing us. I could feel her close to me, some magnetic energy pulling at my skin. I felt her breath on my cheek like a faint night zephyr. She grabbed my right bicep and placed her right hand flat on my chest.

She said, "I'm sorry what happened to you."

I said, "When?"

She giggled and went on. "I can't imagine the fear."

I lurched back and said, "Thank you for the day," and slammed the screen door as I went into the night.

As I drove off, the moon was so bright it lit up the saguaros and ocotillo, the creosote. I thought I heard dogs barking. I stopped and got out and sat on the hood of my car and lit up a Camel. The memory of the dying bulls kept charging into my mind. But instead of matadors, my father kept barging in with a sword, waving it around. I wondered if I was still drunk. I wondered if I'd ever have the chance to touch Kate again. She and Rocco were getting married, or so Rocco said. I flipped the cigarette butt onto the ground and slid off the hood of the car. Somewhere I heard dogs barking.

Brown Sparrows

I paid off the taxi from Oceanside out front of the transient barracks in Camp Pendleton and prepared myself for a life of drab stateside duty.

He was slouched on the front steps of the barracks as I climbed out of the taxi. I knew it was him—skinnier than when we'd been in Staging Battalion together, before going over to Nam—his red hair, his freckles and the wolfish teeth he shot at me when he smiled.

I stretched my cramped legs, threw my sea bag on my shoulder and marched to the barracks steps. Wilson uncoiled and shook my hand. His handshake felt limp just like it did a year ago when we'd met as twenty-year-old gung-ho Marines. Now, as I stared at him, he looked good, like a friend. But I hated that limp handshake and recalled he'd never been my friend.

He said, "Welcome home. I got here yesterday."

I raised my eyebrows and shrugged.

He laughed. "And welcome back to the fucking stateside Corps."

I said, "It's better than the alternative."

He showed me those wolfish teeth through a crooked little smile.

I said, "No time for grab-assing out here. I have to report in."

He nodded. "You're not going to like it."

I stopped. "Why?"

He said, "It doesn't make any difference why. You have

little choice in this man's Corps. I'll be right here when you get checked in. We can go to Oceanside and get some chow, get drunk and commiserate, or do both or none." Right after he said that, he stuck his wide pink tongue out and wagged it around while trying to make his blue eyes go around in a spiral.

Fucking-A, Squeaky—I thought, same old Wilson.

I marched up the steps. Above the double doors hung a small white sign with stenciled red letters. It said, Transient Barracks, Fifth Marine Division, Mainside, Camp Pendleton, California. The building reminded me of ones I'd seen in John Wayne and Richard Widmark movies about World War II; blocky, institutional, painted a dull khaki tint with lots of big windows flashing from both floors. Long wooden stairs ran down in two flights from the four upstairs corners to the green grass planted outside.

I checked in at the admin office and got stationed with Fifth Battalion Recon somewhere out in the middle of fucking nowhere. The enlisted men's club would be too small for any kind of serious drunkenness, the beer wouldn't be cold enough and it wouldn't be Coors, and some lifer NCO club manager would sit around and tattle on us if we got too drunk and badmouthed the Marine Corps. The food in the chow hall would taste like bile and the cooks wouldn't—not couldn't—but wouldn't fry eggs over-easy and we'd have to stomach a lot of shit-on-a-shingle or else starve. Just like being in Nam.

I bitched about having to be in Recon out in the sticks, asked for softer duty, an office pogue posting somewhere, or a supply clerk job, but they didn't care. The lance corporal doing all the talking smirked one of those little grins that said, "Nobody gives a shit what you think."

Irritating music blared from a portable radio atop a credenza behind his desk. It sounded like Frank Sinatra, or one of those other old-fogey singers that all the lifers love.

I said, "You can't do anything better for me?"

I noticed a framed photograph of some four-star general hanging on the wall. He sported a glum expression. I wondered if it was the commandant of the Corps and I realized I didn't even know who the commandant was.

The clerk shrugged and said, "The world needs warriors to do the hard work. And by the way, your new unit will be on standby to go to Nam on very short notice." He smiled, "You're a warrior."

I frowned when I saw the stupid logic of what he said—understood the need for trained killers, not lazy-assed office pogues like him who hung pictures of the commandant on the wall so they could brown-nose the lifers.

I continued to frown because the thought of shipping back to Nam made the inside of my head feel as if it was filling up like a sink, not with water, but with hot blood.

He said, "Tomorrow, they'll send a truck from Camp Horno to fetch you men. Catch a bunk upstairs for the night."

As I toted my sea bag upstairs I knew what Wilson meant when he said, "You won't like it." Meant he was going to Fifth Battalion Recon with me and possibly shipping over to Nam again, too. I wasn't sure if I liked that—being in the same outfit with him again. Even though I'd felt a happy relief upon seeing him.

When I went back outside he was standing close to the same spot sucking on a Newport. I could smell the menthol from twenty feet away. Made me nauseous. I liked Camels—no filters, no menthol, none of that fluffy stuff.

He waved at me as I approached and then started walking towards the street. "Let's get a taxi."

I wasn't sure I wanted to go anywhere with him right then.

He halted at the edge of the asphalt street. We were in a part of the base that had plenty of those old two-story buildings. Hardwood trees clad in a lot of new greenery lined the roads.

When I caught up with him he stood at the curb with

his hand out like he was trying to get someone to stop. He said, "Somebody told me you were up there at Khe Sanh. That true?"

I nodded.

He shook his head and said, "Sorry for you."

I nodded again and looked to the east noticing low hills covered with spring green. There was a lot of traffic—Jeeps, six-bys—driving by, so I couldn't hear what he said after that.

After a couple of minutes I thought I heard him say, "Hold on," as he hailed a cab and stepped into the street.

The cab stopped and Wilson stuck his head in the passenger side window and started talking to the cabby. For the first time I noticed his civvies. Blue shirt to match his eyes and tan trousers way too big for him, his Marine Corps dress shoes spit-shined to mirrors. I laughed. Very similar to what I wore.

He stopped talking to the cabby and looking back at me, asked, "Oceanside?"

I'd heard San Clemente was the best party town and that's where I wanted to go. But I shrugged and said, "Sure."

In the cab he said, "I was with First Battalion, Fifth Marines. A lot of the time around An Hoa and Arizona Territory, then up to Hue."

An eight-track tape player blared and the Young Rascals were singing "Good Lovin'."

I hadn't heard a lot about the Fifth Marines so I figured he'd fought in a war somewhat different from mine. I nodded at him and raised my eyebrows, flattened my lips as if I was impressed.

The music thumped into the floorboard up front and migrated underneath the seat. I could feel it in my feet. Fucking-A, Squeaky, I thought, that's good shit.

They sang about getting some good loving.

Wilson said, "You hard of hearing?"

I said, "Had too many guns go off near me."

The Rascals wailed for a doctor, again and again, as they wondered what was ailing them.

Wilson nodded, "I wasn't at Hue when the shit hit the fan. I was in the snipers at An Hoa and sneaked around the countryside shooting village headmen and politicians suspected of being Cong. We spent a lot of time waiting for targets. I used to get bit by a lot of mosquitoes while I was waiting to split the skull of some unsuspecting gook with a round from my M-14."

More good loving on the tape deck.

He lit another Newport. I moved as far away across the seat as possible and fired up one of my Camels in self defense.

He went on, "And of course, I never took my malaria pills—made me sick."

I gave him that. Made you feel like you weighed a thousand pounds—made your head feel like an oversized grenade.

The eight-track switched songs—"Grooving." But instead of grooving, I fretted about Nam—the soggy heat, the monsoon and all the rest.

Wilson seemed intent on smoking his cigarette—like he'd forgotten I was there. He finally looked at me and said, "So I was in the hospital with malaria, packed in fucking ice when Charlie took Hue and my unit was out there trying to take it back, getting their asses shot off."

I said, "Consider yourself lucky."

He said, "Maybe."

I said, "Maybe, shit."

He said, "I joined the Marine Corps to see some fighting. Real fighting."

I thought, you don't want to know any real fighting.

I said, "Me too."

He nodded, "I admire you for surviving all that combat up there."

I didn't want to think about that. I heard a faint, high-pitched whine in my right ear. I wondered if there was something wrong with the cabby's eight-track.

Wilson stared at me and said, "Did you kill any of those North Vietnamese?"

I stared back into his hard blue eyes.

He barked, "Did you hear what I said?"

I said, "Yeah."

He continued, "I mean, did you kill any gooks where you really knew you blew their asses away?"

I lied. "Hell, yeah."

He put his hand out, palm up and said, "Fucking-A, Marine."

I slapped his palm hard and said, "Fucking-A, Squeaky."

He grinned as he lit another Newport. We both chain-smoked the rest of the way into town.

Downtown, Wilson said to the cabby, "There used to be a good diner just around the corner from the USO. That still there?"

The cabby sniggered, "Nothing changes in this town. Long as we got Marines fighting wars, the businesses will be here to screw them."

Wilson laughed and said, "Nobody screws me."

The cabby mumbled. Wilson continued, "Unless she's beautiful and blonde with big tits."

I saw the cabby roll his eyes in the rear-view mirror as I managed a short, dry laugh.

Inside the diner, we were seated in a booth by a young blonde waitress with big tits. Wilson leered at her but she didn't seem to notice.

The diner walls were painted a tint trapped between khaki and beige. Photos of famous Marines hung above the booths. I recognized John Basilone and the "Fighting Quaker," Lieutenant General Smedley Butler. I remembered his statement, "War is a racket," and thought of Nam and planes shot down and bombs and bullets and bad chow.

General Chesty Puller hung up there, too. His photograph was even autographed. I wondered if he'd really been in this joint. On the other wall I recognized a faded picture of Sergeant Major Dan Dailey. Underneath, taped to the wall, was the challenge he yelled at his Marines in Belleau Wood, "Come on, you sons-of-bitches, do you want to live forever?" I wondered why they had to put that up there.

Wilson said, "So how long you been gone from Vietnam, exactly?"

"I've been in the States twenty-two days and before that in Okinawa for three."

He nodded as he looked at the menu. "So you still got the smell of blood and combat in your nose."

I wasn't sure I did or if I even knew what he was talking about but I stared straight into his eyes and nodded.

We both ordered cheeseburgers and fries with the works and he ordered a Budweiser and so did I because they didn't have Coors on the menu. One of the many things I didn't like about California—no Coors. The waitress didn't believe we were old enough to drink so she carded us. The whole time this went on she didn't smile once. I couldn't tell if she was mad at Wilson for staring at her tits or if it was something else. Maybe she was just plain sick of young Marines always checking out her big knockers.

While we waited for our chow Wilson started flipping through the menu on the jukebox station at our booth.

"Ah, a new Van Morrison song."

Van Morrison didn't ring a bell.

He looked at me and said, "Brown Eyed Girl."

I stared out the front window as he dug some money out of his trouser pockets. A large silver-tinted light post stood at attention in front of the window. Beyond that, I spotted a line of brown sparrows, eight or nine of them, across the street on the telephone line. They looked like a jury or that lineup of famous Marine photos on the wall or something.

Then I saw them start to flit around like they were anxious.

Wilson said, "I love Van Morrison. Don't you?"

I shrugged and looked for the waitress. She stood at the small window between the dining room and the kitchen waiting for the cook to pass her some plates of chow. I noticed her legs. She had muscled calves and her thighs looked hard. She moved a little and glared at me.

Wilson said, "You don't like "Gloria?""

I frowned, wondered if that was the waitress' name and how he'd know that.

He said, "You don't like G-L-O-R-I-A?"

"Aha," I said, "that was by Them."

He said, "Yeah. Them. And Van Morrison was the lead singer."

Just then the song came on and I liked it. Fucking-A, Squeaky, I really liked it. It sounded like all the good Beatles, Rolling Stones, Dave Clark Five, Young Rascals and Spencer Davis Trio music rolled up together and improved on. I felt the beat of it coming through the floor and up into my feet. I fancied the pictures on the walls could hear the rock and roll and grumpy old General Chesty Puller boogy-ing out to that song.

The waitress brought the food as Wilson crammed more quarters into the jukebox choosing number A9, "Brown Eyed Girl."

When the waitress put our big white plates on the table I noticed she had brown eyes, the color of the furry, four-legged vermin that inhabited our bunkers at Khe Sanh—beautiful brown. I smiled at the thought of her brown eyes and that song blaring out of the jukebox and maybe she knew that or maybe she just liked the fact that I smiled at her because she sort of smiled, too—she tried to hide it, but she smiled.

Juice oozed out of the cheeseburgers and the fat dripped down our chins as we ate and the ketchup on the French fries got all over the bone-white plates. We wiped our faces a lot and chased our burgers with cold sips of beer, rocking to Van Morrison and glancing at the waitress. I caught her staring at us and when I did she quickly managed to find something else to look at. The inside of my chest fluttered.

Somebody got tired of "Brown Eyed Girl" and played some country shit with a lot of twangy guitar and whining. Wilson looked at my white plate smeared with the blood-red ketchup and said, "A lot of killing up there at Khe Sanh, no?"

I nodded. "I don't want to talk about it."

He said, "Okay, we won't talk about it."

Brown Eyed Girl brought our check and sauntered away.

I used my head to motion towards the table, "You get the tip," as I started to grab the check.

He laughed, "No way, asshole. Brown Eyed Girl is mine. You leave the tip."

I shrugged and threw a dollar on the table, then walked out. As I did, I smiled at the waitress but she was intent on taking his money. I glanced at the photos of Smedley and Chesty and Dan Daley and almost saluted as I walked out.

Outside, I fired up a Camel. Even though it was spring, the evening air had a fall-like quality to it, the light coming in sideways, illuminating the walls of the buildings across the street a soft amber color.

A yellow Volkswagon sped past. Through her open window I saw a young blonde woman and she looked like she had big tits. At the first cross street she flipped a u-turn and gunned her engine. I stepped back a bit as she aimed that yellow Bug at an empty parking space in front of where I stood.

Wilson stomped out and said, "I asked her out but she just frowned."

I nodded, but kept my eyes on the big-titted blonde in the yellow Bug. Camel smoke drifted into my eyes and burned them. Instead of slowing down, the Bug sped up. I wondered if she had stepped on the gas by mistake.

The yellow VW smashed into the big silver light pole right in front of Wilson and me, and the blonde shot head first over the steering wheel, which shattered into pieces, then through the windshield, which also shattered. The racket reminded me of a burning C-130 slamming into red ground. She clanged head first into the light pole. Even I heard that.

My knees sagged. Two or three people on the street, including Wilson, ran to her side. They talked fast but I couldn't hear what they said. The only thing I heard was a swooshing like the imminent arrival of rocket rounds.

Wilson looked up and waived for me to advance but I just stared at him. He grimaced. Somebody ran to the door of the restaurant and screamed, "Call an ambulance."

I backed up and wilted against the restaurant window. People were running across the street towards the wreck with that look in their eyes. The look you see in the eyes of men when they become aware you are just about to shoot them.

I heard Wilson take charge. He gave a lot of orders, but I couldn't tell you what the words were. I thought of Smedley Butler and Chesty giving orders and Dan Daley yelling about living forever.

Brown Eyed Girl ran out the door and glared at me as she passed and knelt next to Wilson. She handed him a pile of clean white cloths.

I heard sirens. On the telephone line across the street I noticed the sparrows I had seen while eating. They fluttered around, up and down, their furious little wings flapping. They looked like they were in combat—then they mated. I laughed. Before, they'd reminded me of a corporate board meeting or something—all lined up. But hell, now the telephone wire looked like a whorehouse.

Two cop cars and an ambulance arrived. There was a lot of shouting, "Get back. Make way. Get back."

Wilson and the waitress backed up. I noticed they were standing close. He tried to capture her hand. Right then I felt like I had a pit inside my guts that went all the way through the earth to Khe Sanh.

Wilson looked at her. His eyes had the excitement that unexpected death brings. She was crying. She suddenly looked back at me with one of those looks that says, "Come on."

I stood tall and marched through the gathering crowd as the ambulance driver bent over the victim. I strode to a spot where I got a good look at the body. I noticed the blonde victim's hands, delicate arms and face were the color of the white plates we had eaten from, blood smeared around like swirls of ketchup.

I must have fallen down, because suddenly Wilson cradled my head in his hands. His blue eyes seemed like beacons that flash in the dead and misty Vietnam night.

He said, "Hey man, it's all right."

My head spun. I tried to smile.

He lifted my head and I saw those sparrows furiously fornicating on the telephone line across the street, and I laughed. I looked at Wilson and he reminded me of Dan Daley's photo—valiant, glum, valiant—I couldn't imagine anything more hilarious—I laughed harder.

He said, "What's so funny?"

Brown Eyed Girl stood over him. She seemed concerned. I suddenly heard that damned song in my head.

He said, "What's so fucking funny?"

I couldn't tell him. The words would not form. I heard Van Morrison singing over the high thin whine in my right ear. He sang about going somewhere on the days that the rain came. I wanted to scream because suddenly I couldn't see those fucking sparrows from where I was. I only saw them in my mind. When they fornicated it looked like fighting. I laughed louder.

He pulled my head to his chest and said, "It's all right."

Fucking-A, Squeaky, they were fornicating. They were singing, Squeaky, they were fighting.

Brig Duty

The assistant brig warden sent us to the shrink to see if we were fit to work in the brig. Me and Smith and Bailey. We went down there with Sergeant Lyle.

In the dispensary, the cement deck was painted red, waxed and buffed. Light from the fluorescents glowed softly in the floor shine; looked like little white spots. Somewhere a buffer hummed.

After Lyle left, Bailey said, "That guy's an asshole."

Bailey needed a shave. He was already losing his hair, too.

Smith said, "Yeah, how about yesterday, when he slammed that prisoner's face into the wall?"

I looked out the window at the bushes. Dust smothered the leaves of the loquat. Needed rain. I thought about Lyle. He'd wiped the prisoner's blood off his hands with a white handkerchief. He'd gotten blood on his shoes, too. He growled at the Duck prisoner, made him get on his knees and wipe it off.

Bailey said, "Yeah, that fucker's been here too long. Maybe they should send him back to Nam for some attitude adjustment. See what it's really like."

Smith said, "What's really like?"

Bailey laughed, "The world, numby. Not here in San Diego where they lock Ducks up just for not wanting to be in the Navy. Then order us to guard them."

Smith said, "Oh, yeah. I know what you mean."

Bailey said, "Who the fuck wants to be in the Navy?"

Smith said, "Not me."

I said, "What the hell you doing in the Marines? That's part of the Navy."

Smith said, "If I'd known what Marines were like, I'd never signed on. Would have gone Air Force."

Bailey said, "Well, whatever. I don't know if I cotton to babysitting Ducks who don't want to be in the Navy."

Smith said, "Me neither."

I watched the corpsmen hustle around us in the hallway as they carried hypodermic needles and handfuls of gauze pads. Their blue dungarees seemed old, no creases where they ought to be.

Bailey tapped his foot, said, "When we going to see this shrink?"

Smith said, "Hope it's soon."

Bailey said, "What rank is a shrink, captain or something?"

A Duck walked down the hall. Older than us. His shoes clicked on the hard-buffed floor. He had one of those looks lifers get. One of those fuck-you looks. He stopped and sneered. Bailey sneered back. Smith looked at the buffed red floor. The lifer said, "Who's Peters?"

I said, "Me, Chief."

"Get your ass down there and see Lieutenant Jones."

I said, "Aye, aye, Chief."

As we walked away I heard Bailey hiss, "Aye, aye, Chief, my ass."

I followed the chief to a closed door that said, "Base Psychiatrist."

The chief nodded at me and walked away. I knocked on the door. It felt hard on my knuckles.

A voice said, "Enter."

I opened the door. A young heavy-set man dressed in Navy khakis sat staring at me. His curly black hair needed cutting. He tapped a sharpened pencil on the sheet of glass covering his desktop.

I said, "Corporal Peters reporting as ordered, Sir."

He waved his limp hand. I was reminded of bored history teachers.

He said, "Sit, Peters."

I said, "Aye, aye, Sir."

I sat on a hardwood chair. He leaned back and crossed his left leg over his knee, swiveled in his chair, continuing to drum his pencil on the glass.

Behind him the drapes were open. Naval officers slouched around a picnic table in an atrium. One of them had on a blue ball cap that said "USS Kitty Hawk" across the front. They drank Cokes and laughed, slapped their hands on the table's top and on each others' backs. They all wore aviator's wings on their chests.

The shrink said, "I see you just got back from across the pond."

"Yes, Sir. Four months back. Transferred in here from a recon unit."

His pencil lead rapped on the glass top.

I wondered what all those aviators were doing at the dispensary. Maybe in for their annual eyesight checkups.

The shrink said, "See a lot of combat?"

In the atrium one of the Duck lieutenants jumped up and spread his arms like an airplane. He began to run around like he was flying. The other officers laughed.

Louder, the shrink said, "Kill a few gooks?"

I looked at him for a long time. Noticed the single ribbon—the fire watch ribbon—that stood out on his chest like an A-plus on a report card. I couldn't answer him. I looked at my chest, my ribbons; three rows. I looked at his hand drumming the pencil, could almost make out the reflection of his face in the sheet of glass.

He said, "How you feel about guarding these sailors?"

I said, "Fine, Sir."

He nodded. Outside, the officer acting like an airplane crashed against a pillar. His face was red and his teeth gleamed as he laughed. I could hear the others laughing, too. Came right through the glass window.

Staring out the window at the aviators, the shrink said, "OK, Marine. You're cleared for duty."

I stood at attention.

Without looking at me, he said, "Dismissed."

Walking down the hall my shoes clicked on the hard red floor. The color made me think of blood; semi-dried blood.

I remembered the plane crash. C-130 came in over the gooks' trenchline. Bastards lit it up, ack-ack and rockets. Flamed an engine. It flew like a quail that'd been shot on the wing.

Down the hall Bailey sat bent at the waist looking at the floor. Lost in some daydream. I snorted when I noticed the light reflecting off his balding head. Smith stared through the glass windows.

After the plane got hit, it somehow got to the firebase and sat down on the runway, but it wasn't stopping, not on any command of some Duck pilot. It kept coming. At us. I felt like running, but didn't know where, just wanted to hide. I stood there. Nobody else ran. The plane turned sideways, kept sledding.

I thought I could hear those Navy pilots in the atrium laughing. And the sneer on that shrink's face, jumbled with sounds of metal scraping runway. It made me want to go back and slap that shrink's face. Slap his silly little fire-watch-ribbon face until it turned bright red. And those Duck aviators outside. With their aviator's wings. In the atrium.

The plane finally came to a stop, its props still turning. It was resting off the runway, in the old ammo dump. The one the gooks blew all to hell. A blast shook the plane and fire roared up like tongues of great tigers. Ordnance cooked off inside. Willy-peter smoke, white as oblivion, burned my nose. Men tried escaping out the rear of the plane. Like sulfur-headed matches with legs. They flared, fell and rolled; flailed their arms. And somebody kicked out the window of the pilot's cockpit and men hung down and fell to the ground. Must have been twenty-five, thirty feet.

Bailey looked up as I approached. I could see his three rows of ribbons, a Bronze Star, two Purple Hearts. I nodded as I walked by on my way to find Sergeant Lyle.

Sand Pebbles

We went up on the roof of the barracks and smoked a couple of joints. The weed was trash but was all we could get.

McGinty said, "Let's go see the movie."

I said, "What is it?"

Carlyle said, "Something called *Sand Pebbles*."

I said, "What's it about?"

Carlyle said, "Steve McQueen's a Duck in the movie. Something about China, in the thirties, I think." He squinted through his thick glasses when he said that. He always squinted when he talked.

Petry grinned.

I coughed on a big hit that burned down to the bottom of my lungs. It made my stomach want to come up. Inside out. I had to lean over and hold my chest. I winced with pain.

Petry grinned.

Carlyle said, "Something about a Duck gunboat on the Yangtze River."

McGinty hummed and stared at the little slip of moon that hung low in the eastern sky

Petry smiled at me and shook his head.

I said, "What's so funny?"

He said, "Nothing."

We walked downstairs. McGinty and Carlyle were talking loud about Chinese and Steve McQueen.

Outside, the sun slung low hemmed in by clouds that looked like exhaust remains from all the ship traffic in the bay. Behind the building that housed the theater, and the building where the transient barracks were, I could see the cranes and elevators where the ships docked. The smell of algae and stale salt water, the thud of diesel, scent of steel-gray deck paint, and the whoosh of jet fighters swooping overhead.

There was a line of people waiting in front of the theater. Waiting to buy tickets. They looked like stick people as we approached. Petry's boots clocked on the hard concrete walk. The people stood still, not moving. I wondered if they were alive. Somebody finally stirred.

We walked to the end of the line. I stared at the people just to our front. Looked like a Navy officer and his family. He was wearing civvies, but I could tell. They have a way. Probably a boat driver who brought his ship in for repairs. Meeting the family for some entertainment. The wife looked good. Was wearing a tight blue skirt. Two girls, probably high school-aged. Their breasts stood out on their chests. Like they were proud of them. The girls stared at us. At me. One had eyes that reminded me of cows that Dad had run out on the flats below the high mountains. The eyes were large and brown, luminous. She stared at me. I felt a bead of sweat down my back. She smiled. I smiled back, then turned and spoke to Petry who was looking up at the moon.

I said, "What's to it?"

He said, "Wow. The moon. Look."

I looked up and saw a thin sickle. Inside the arc of the sickle a bright star and contrails from a jet that had just passed.

I said, "Wow," then elbowed Carlyle. I said, "McGinty. Check out the moon."

I didn't take my eyes off the sight, but felt McGinty and Carlyle look up. We stared. It seemed like a long time. Petry said, "Wow," twice.

Someone behind coughed and I looked at them. Two sailors in their dress whites grinned like they knew something I didn't. I glanced around. The line had moved on. We stood by ourselves in a little knot, isolated, the line in front moving through to buy tickets, the line behind patiently waiting for us to wake up. I looked at the girls; they were smiling at us and shooting us curious looks. Occasionally their eyes shot to the officer, who kept looking back and frowning at us. I kicked Petry, said, "We better move along."

Inside the theater, we bought some popcorn and Cokes, except for Petry. He bought a root beer. We stood in the aisle trying to decide where to sit. The walls seemed to close in. People moved around us, a hubbub, words out of nowhere like, "Nineteen-thirty," "Communists," "Chiang Kai-Shek," "Dumb-ass Marines," "Get out of the way."

The theater had two blocks of seats. The block closest to the screen was filling up. No one sat in the back block. I sat in the front row of the back block. Felt like I had some space if I needed to move fast. Get away. We listened; whispers, crunching kernels, ice in Cokes, feet shuffling, sighs.

The movie started. It was a jumble of wide river and Chinese in traditional garb, river boats and whorehouses with American sailors and Chinese girls. Then Steve McQueen was trying to teach a Chinese guy how to understand the steam engine of a gunboat, and he was understanding, and the sailors hated that, a Chinese man who could understand. The sailors hated Steve McQueen, who'd become a Jonah, causing bad luck with his helping Chinese men learn to be twentieth-century. He got in a fight over the Chinese man in the engine room and then he bet all his money that the little Chinese man could beat the big, mean American sailor in a fight. In a bar, and screaming and lots of cash, bloody noses. Petry laughed, then Carlyle and McGinty.

Petry said, "Wow."

I looked around, saw people in the dark theater. They

looked at us. We were laughing, sweat on the fat man's bare belly, bloody nose and lips of the Chinese. The little Chinese man beat the big, mean American sailor. We laughed harder. The officer with the good-looking wife in the tight blue skirt and two daughters with their breasts standing out proud frowned. On the screen, angry captains and fights over whores with faces like angels and lots of Asian unrest and politics; just like Nam, Commies and good guys mixing it up. The bad guys in the street, yelling at us (American sailors), rioting, chasing us, their red banners and Chinese flags.

We laughed at the turmoil, made us think of Nam, or it did me anyway. Made me think of helping people, and them not understanding we were helping them.

Then rioters chased the sailors out of brothels, and people shouted unintelligible syllables and the Chinese man ran to get on the ship. The one in the engine room ran from the bad guys, and I laughed because that's not how it is. Helping people, I mean. They don't understand. The bad men caught the Chinese man from the engine room and tied his hands behind his back. I thought, we are just trying to help.

Carlyle was laughing, and McGinty. The bad guys hoisted the Chinese man from the engine room on a tripod. He dangled like a steer carcass. It's not like that, you don't have to hate him just because he's helping us. We're all helping each other. I laughed at the absurdity of the hate. The bad men pointed swords at the sailors on the ship and yelled things in Chinese, and the sailors acted like they didn't understand. I laughed and understood the sailors didn't understand. I didn't either, and I laughed at the incongruity, and then the bad guys began to cut big swaths on the muscled chest of the Chinese man from the engine room, and blood dripped and McQueen looked baffled, and we laughed. Then the Chinese man screamed for someone to kill him and we laughed, "Yes, yes kill him."

I thought, no one understands but him; kill him, kill him before the people who don't understand cut him to pieces, a little at a time, and Steve McQueen took a rifle and shot the man, and we laughed. McGinty and Petry were bent over, their faces red, and Carlyle with a big smile. My belly hurt, and I tried to stop, but it was like trying to cram hate back down that had to come up. So I laughed, and suddenly we stopped because everyone was looking at us, and the two girls, their eyes wide, looked like they had just seen something they never wanted to see again. The theater was dead quiet except for the voices screaming Chinese in the movie.

Petry said, "Wow."

They were watching us. I felt like the whole world was watching me.

From the screen, Steve McQueen was looking out at us. Shock gripped his face. The whole world was watching.

Party

Mingo didn't like it but Wiley and I ate acid anyway. We respected him enough to drop it early and get over the rushes and paranoia. On the way to Mingo's we babbled about the war. Conflict. When we got there we were cruising on combat highway; images of sandbags, scent of blood.

Mingo left his old lady in bed with a dose of mono and the three of us walked through the alleys down by the bay. Party time. Fog rode our backs like flak jackets.

Mingo looked at me, "Whatever you do, don't talk about the fucking war. Nobody wants to hear that shit. Bums them out."

Red trails like tracer rounds chased the words out of his mouth.

Wiley said, "I ain't going to rap."

Mingo glared. Great splotches glowed below his cheekbones. It reminded me of the night sky around Khe Sanh when flares backlit the cold mist I grinned.

Mingo frowned, said, "What about you, shithead?"

I smiled. The war was in my throat; the need to shout it out. I thought I'd bust wide open

At the party, Wiley and I sat on a big sofa. Mingo wandered off to hustle some free love. Women walked by in short skirts; the angles on their faces lit by black lights. Harsh. Like cadavers.

The host sat, asked, "What's to it?"

Wiley nodded.

I said, "Nothing to it."

The host said, "Who you guys?"

I said, "We're here with Mingo."

He said, "You in the Corps, too?"

I nodded. The war was in my mouth, right behind my teeth. It wanted out. I thought I'd vomit.

The host allowed a tepid grin. He started to walk. I grabbed his arm. "Yeah, man. I was at Khe Sanh. Seventy-seven days of pure shit."

Lights spun. Beads clicked. The host nodded, looked away.

I said, "Those fucking gooks tried to blast our asses."

He craned his neck, searched for somebody.

I said, "You know how many guys died out of our company?"

He caught Mingo's eye. Wiley watched the women stroll by.

I said, "Sixty-six. Sixty-six KIAs out of one-hundred and forty men, man. World War I shit."

Mingo charged over, eyes like lenses on a gas mask.

I said, "One fucking patrol, man. Ninety-nine casualties. We all got hit, man. All of us." I started to show him my scars.

Mingo hissed in my ear.

I said, "Wait, wait, man. I'm fucking lucky. Like I was impossible to kill."

Mingo said, "Shut the fuck up. Nobody gives a fuck." His face twisted. "You're bumming me out, man."

I let the host go. Wiley giggled for a long time. I looked at the women, too. I could see through their dresses. There was nothing there.

Christmas Night

The headlights on the farm road looked like a bright tunnel. Sandy drifts crunched under tires. Wetback housing festooned with Christmas lights stood out in the cold mist like harbingers of faith.

I drove fast. Fiver rode shotgun. Step and Rat sat in the back. Jimi Hendrix blared out of the eight-track and rolled around the inside of the car. Like water in a toilet bowl, the swish before evacuation. Fiver said, "Pinto's place. His old lady split. Ain't nobody there. The key's underneath the welcome mat."

I said, "Where'd the old lady go?"

Step said, "To mama."

I nodded and took a sip of Bud.

Step said, "I forgot, Farley. You used to be sweet on her. Before Pinto knocked her up."

A coyote crossed the road. Light beamed off his eyes. A bright gold. I waited for something to rear up inside me in response to Step, but nothing showed in my head.

Fiver turned in his seat, watching the coyote. He said, "That doggie looks like the fucking devil."

Step said, "You got your gun?"

I said, "Yeah."

Step said, "Turn around and we'll kill that coyote."

Fiver said, "No. We got urgent business."

Fiver turned and looked at Rat. "You got the works?"

Rat nodded.

A white house trailer reflected light.

Step said, "There it is. If his old lady was there we could spark her. Huh, Farley?"

I looked into the rearview mirror. Noticed Step's crooked teeth. Fiver chuckled.

Step said, "That piss you off, Farley?"

My stomach burned.

Fiver said, "Lighten up, Step. She's a foxy chick. I don't blame Farley for wanting to sniff up her flank."

I slowed, pulled off the road and parked in front of the trailer. Fiver looked around, motioned with his head. We stepped out, pulled our jackets tight and walked to the stoop. Fiver lifted the mat and found the key, fumbled with the handle, opened the door and stepped in. A light switched on and he looked out, nodded for us to come in.

I walked into the front room. It was mostly empty and smelled of cat piss. Thin beige curtains hung over white window shades. A picture of a smiling Jesus lit up by rays from Heaven hung on one wall, a Sacred Heart hung opposite. It looked like someone had carved it. One of the local wetback farm hands. Bread crumbs mixed with mouse turds covered the kitchen table.

Fiver said to Rat, "I got the shit. Get your spoon and let's cook some."

I walked down a long hall. Snapped on a light, saw a filled-up waterbed in the room at the end. The blankets and sheets were gone. I imagined her in it. Step moved up behind and whispered in my ear, "That's where Pinto slammed it to her. A lot, I'll bet. All that time you were in Nam. She was putting out for lots of guys."

I turned and pushed past Step. At the table Rat had a lighter going under a blackened spoon. Fiver stretched a piece of plastic tubing. A hypodermic needle lay on the table. A bag full of white powder.

Fiver said, "We got number-one crystal. Call it Black Widow." He spread those last two words way out.

I stared at the needle then looked at the picture of Jesus.

Step said, "Pinto's old lady fucked a lot of people. Didn't care. Even when she was married to Pinto. I heard she fucked you, Fiver. That true?"

I shot a glance at Fiver.

Fiver spread his hands wide. ' Not me, motherfucker. Not me. Don't mess with hitched women. Good way to end up dead."

Rat nodded and Fiver picked up the hypodermic. He stuck the needle into the hot liquid in the spoon and filled the hypodermic barrel. He looked up at me and smiled, "Ever do speed?"

"No."

Fiver said, "Really. I thought all you fuckers in Nam did heavy shit."

I said. "Nope. Killing's serious business."

Fiver grinned. "Come on, let's get high."

I shrugged and pulled off my jacket, dropped it on the floor. It clunked. Step looked at the jacket then narrowed his eyes. I smiled as I rolled up my sleeve.

Fiver said, "Put your arm over here."

Fiver put the rubber tubing around my upper forearm and twisted it tight. He said, "Now Farley, pump your fist."

As I pumped my fist I stared at Step. Step smiled, his crooked teeth showing hints of tartar.

Fiver said, "Great veins. Rat, hit him up."

I had to admit, my forearm looked like chiseled stone. Rat picked up the hypodermic and gently pierced a bulging vein. His long nose nearly touched my arm. Blood registered in the hypodermic barrel. It swirled a deep red in the liquid speed. I watched Step as Rat slowly injected the liquid into my veins. My eyelids closed and I slumped.

Fiver said, "Good shit, huh?"

Rat pulled the needle out of my arm. I swayed as I rolled down my shirtsleeve, then walked over and picked up my jacket and put it on. Step watched me the whole time. I lay on the floor and stuffed my hands in the jacket pockets and felt the pistol's cold barrel.

Rat shot up Fiver and Step, then himself. They sat on the floor, quiet. Then Fiver got up and went out to the car. Step went with him. The sound of doors opening and closing cut through the silence. Fiver came in with four beers. Hendrix playing "Voodoo Child" drifted in my head. Fiver handed a Bud to each of us. I opened mine and took a sip, then closed my eyes.

Step came in and said, "Where's your piece, Farley?"

I opened my eyes and looked at him.

Fiver got up and started to pace, then said, "We need some music. Too bad the old lady took everything."

Step said, "Everything but the waterbed. The scene of the crimes." He cackled as he kicked my right foot.

Fiver strummed air guitar, his voice mimicking Eric Clapton playing "Sunshine of Your Love." He spread his short legs and lifted his head and belted out off-tune notes. He shook his long hair. Rat giggled.

Fiver said, "Come on fuckers, let's party."

Step said, "Yeah, let's go find Pinto's old lady. I hear she pulls trains."

I got up, walked up to Step and stopped, put my face up close and looked into his eyes.

Step said, "What you going to do about it, fuckhead?"

I felt like I was levitated three feet off the floor as I pulled my .38 Special out of my pocket and pointed it at Step. He jumped back, his eyes suddenly large. He knocked his beer over.

Fiver said, "Don't be breaking bad, motherfuckers."

I twirled the pistol like I was an old-time gun hand and walked to the door. I turned the knob and pointed the pistol at Step's face again and smiled as I sighted down the short barrel.

Step said, "Hey man, I was just fucking around."

I said, "I notice you didn't say she'd fucked you."

Step said, "Not me, man. Never touched her."

I pulled the hammer back on the pistol. Step fell back against the wall, his mouth open like he wanted to yell something but forgot what it was. I took a deep breath then let it out as I squeezed the trigger. The hammer struck the firing pin and a tepid click echoed off the walls. I laughed and jammed the pistol in my jacket pocket. I looked at the Sacred Heart, crossed myself, stepped outside and closed the door.

Inside my body, I was streaking like a dead man's soul headed for purgatory. Far off, on someone's farm, I noticed a big cottonwood draped with Christmas lights that twinkled in the dark.

Tit For Tat

Mimi sneaked in. She probably thought I couldn't hear her. But I couldn't sleep because my head hurt like somebody had jammed a spike through the frontal lobe. Damaged, it spun from excess Crown Royal and cans of Coors, but I still heard her. Or maybe I didn't hear her, but I sure as hell smelled her. Stale cigarette smoke tangled up inside that kinky, big-haired permanent she paid so much for.

My first thought was, she quit smoking three years ago, and then I figured she must have partied at some honky-tonk and no telling where else.

We had planned to go out, but I got loaded frying up bull nuts for the East Side Cotton Farmers' monthly barbeque. I stayed there all day, slicing bull gonads and slamming shots of Crown Royal and making sure the fire built enough mesquite coals. I couldn't do anything when I got home but crash, so I can't say as I blame her for doing me a tit for tat. Just as long's that's all it was, just a tit for tat.

Sleep failed to arrive after she came home. The cigarette stench conjured images of honky-tonk bands, tall, skinny bass players with slouchy cowboy hats, the brims rolled up too tight against the sides of the crown, and booze-induced pickup wrecks after everybody left the bar to stagger home. Plus I fretted about where the hell else she'd been besides dancing the Cotton-eyed Joe with a bunch of ogling cowboys intent on getting in her knickers.

So next morning my head swelled like an overripe watermelon due to a lack of sleep, plus all the fun frying bull nuts from the day before. But I was up and just finishing a mug of tepid, day-old javvy infused with a shot of Crown Royal—a little hair of the dog that bit me—when I heard Darnell's pickup truck rumble out front of my house. I hurried outside because he'd want to hammer on the door at five-thirty in the morning or ring the doorbell twenty-five times. Just to irritate Mimi.

He'd send her into a tizzy faster than anybody I know. Sometimes he'd say, "Want to make out?" Times like that her basalt-black eyes bored a hole through him as he chuckled. The lobes of her ears turned red, too, and every once in a while she tried to kick him in the nuts. He'd har-har it and stick his tongue out at her and that was a sight to see, that tongue—seemed as long as my forearm and damned near as wide. When he stuck that thing out the women would make a face like they'd handled a rattle-snake or something worse and then frown as if they'd witnessed the ugliest thing in all of Arizona, and God knows, Darnell is one ugly man.

I crept out the front door, climbed into his truck before he caused problems and as he pulled onto the street and revved his engine a time or two he grinned at me. I noticed a couple of electric cattle prods and a whip hanging on a rack between the seat back and the rear window.

I said, "Don't start your shit."

"What shit?"

"Waking the damned neighborhood up."

He said, "Settle down, Marvin."

I said, "I got to live here. You don't."

"Aw, hell, it ain't nothing."

I said, "It will be something if you wake Mimi up."

He laughed. "That's what I was trying to do. I reckon she don't feel so hot."

I said, "What do you know?"

He smiled, "Plenty."

"Like what?"

"Ah, hell, Marvin, you don't need to worry. She was fine."

"You see her last night?"

He cackled again, "Hell, yes, I danced with her."

That bothered me. He stuck a fat Roi Tan Banker in his mouth and chewed the end off, then spat it on the floor of the truck. Mimi tries not to pay Darnell any attention.

I said, "Who else?"

He said, "Settle down." Then he said, "She was okay. She behaved." As he chewed that cigar it reminded me of a hard missile or some other kind of prod.

I nodded and watched the highway as we headed for the penitentiary. His headlights reached out and found the jack rabbits darting alongside the pavement and once, right after we left town, a high-yellow coyote hurrying across the road. I figured that if Mimi was around Darnell, I shouldn't be worried because he's so damned ugly and I know how Mimi feels about him, but then I thought about him and his stupid fat tongue and what he might know how to do with it. When I glanced at him he used it to lick the shank of that damned stinking Roi-Tan.

Once, years ago, I asked him if he'd ever done it with her. He frowned and shook his head, then laughed a hard, dry laugh as he retorted, "I don't want to die." Later, when I thought about it, I wondered if he meant me killing him for doing it with her or her killing him for even trying.

He reached under the seat and pulled out an empty coffee mug and handed it to me. I looked at his broad, flat face and he smiled.

He handed me the thermos and said, "Want a cup?"

I didn't know what I was getting, but nodded.

He pitched me the thermos and as soon as I cracked the lid the scent of strong javvy penetrated my nose, jolted the inside of my brain. I poured a cup—I knew it was going to be strong and bitter.

I looked at him and blurted, "Did you fuck her?"

He looked at me like I'd stabbed him with a knife. "Who?"
I said, "My old lady?"

His big lips spread into a wide smile as he let out a big
har-har although I didn't think it too damned funny. As he
laughed he reached under the seat again and pulled out a
bottle of Dewar's and said, "Here, put a snort of this Scotch
in your coffee and no I did not fuck her."

I cracked the seal on the top of the bottle and poured
one glug, two glugs, three glugs and then he yelled, "Hey,
knock it off with all the Scotch. We got a job to do. The
State don't want to pay us for a bunch of bad work."

I grinned, "Why not?"

He said, "They want to get a calf crop and if we get drunk
right now we'll ..."

I said, "That ain't what I'm talking about."

He yelled, "Marvin! She don't like me—at least good
enough to shuck her jeans and let me lick her. Besides, you
need to get this fucking business straight in your head—
it's just biological. Cats and dogs do it. Sex is only tied to
love if you make it that way." He leaned over and put his
face closer, "Biological, Marvin, b-i-o-l-o-g-i-c-a ..."

I swiped an open hand at his faced and missed as I said,
"It's more than that to me."

He spread one of those exasperated looks across his face
and leaned back into his seat.

I took a sip of the coffee/Scotch concoction and the bite
of it jangled my spine.

He said, "Quit worrying about who's trying to get in your
wife's pants."

"Why?"

"Because you're going to make yourself crazy and besides why the hell you hitched to her if all you worry about
is who she's fucking besides you?"

"Don't you worry about your wife?"

He looked at me and shook his head, "For somebody
who's supposed to be so almighty intelligent, you sure

are a dumb ass. Trust, Marvin." He sucked on the Roi Tan Banker and the lit end grew fiery red, then subsided. He took it out of his mouth and waved it around as he went on, "Learn to trust."

I attempted another sip and this time the taste didn't make me gag.

He said, "Listen up, I need to change the subject. The State ain't paying me for any misses, so we got to be careful about our work. If the cows don't get knocked up, they won't hire me to do the work next year."

I nodded and watched tall cottonwood trees lining the side of the highway.

He went on. "I know you got A. I. certified from the junior college, but performing artificial insemination on real cows in a real herd is a different matter altogether."

A hint of sun sent a pale light into the bottom of the eastern sky.

"Those prison-herd Holsteins are old cows. They got crooked cervixes and they're savvy about humans sticking their arms up their asses and insemination tubes into their uteruses. They kick and they fight. Your forearm's going to be sore as hell when we get through. If you get tired, say something and I'll take over." He hacked up a lunger and spat it on the floor of the truck. I glared at him.

"If I have to take over, though, I ain't going to pay you for the ones I have to breed."

I decided not to look at him and watched his windshield, all the dead bug guts accumulated there.

He went on, "I don't think you'll have too much of a problem. They won't be that bad. I mean, they'll be easier to inseminate than heifers, but still it will be a chore."

I thought about insemination, the semen inserted into the uterus, the fight the semen face to penetrate the egg, the odds that it even happens—pregnancy—the odds, pretty amazing.

He reached under the seat and pulled out a paper bag

which he tossed at me. "Get them hats out."

I reached into the bag and pulled out two red ball caps. The flat bills told me they were brand new.

He nodded. "Go ahead on. Put one on." He rolled down his window, leaned his head into the wind and turning it slightly, spat out a mouthful of tobacco juice. He went on, "Let's review the process of how you inseminate a cow, okay?"

I looked at the white tags inside the hats, trying to cipher the sizes, could barely read them and tried not to react to Darnell's last statement. One of the tags read seven-and-a-quarter, the other seven-and-three-quarters. I took the smaller one. I didn't think I needed a lecture on inseminating cows but let it ride. I tossed him the larger hat because Darnell's head is like his tongue, and his mouth for that matter—oversized.

He said, "You going to respond?"

I frowned. "I don't think I need to talk about any of that ..."

He smiled and resumed as if I hadn't spoken, "Remember, getting the tube inside the vestibule of the vagina is the easy part."

I watched the road run away from us as if we were driving in a tunnel and thought, that's the hardest part with Mimi.

"You got to be able to feel that vagina with the left hand that you have stuck inside the rectum." He leaned over and leered, "I think that's the part they hate the most, the hand up their ass."

A dark-tinted night bird—a nighthawk or small owl— flitted across the boundary where dark meets headlight shine.

I looked at the decal sewn on the front of the hat I held. The patch's background was black with a red logo that read, "ABS." Underneath in thin white thread it read, "American Breeders Service." I liked the look of that hat. I worked the edges of the bill and thought, I look good in red.

He said, "Getting from the softness of the vagina into the cervix is the most work." He took a sip of his coffee and after he swallowed, hacked like it burned his esophagus. "The cervix is hard and in these old cows it might be crooked, or cracked, not a straight shot into paradise like a man would think."

The low light from the dash of the truck shone on his face in ambers and reds that lit up the bottom side of his chin.

"You can usually run your left hand a little farther up the ass and feel that cervix and just on the other end you can feel the soft spot where the uterus starts. You gotta have the feel for it to do it all the time, for a living I mean. Once you get the business end of the plastic tube through the cervix and into the uterus you can squeeze that bulb on the other end and let the semen do their job of knocking up that old cow."

He said, "While we're at it, we need to preg test them cows because that crazy veterinarian over there may have gotten his hands on some semen and inseminated them already. I paid ten dollars a pop for that bull jism in the back of the truck. If we don't need it, we don't use it. Got that?"

I wondered how much he would pay me for all this extra work I suddenly had to do.

Seemed he anticipated me, "We'll settle up about that later today."

I said, "Is the vet from Florence going to meet us there?"

"Naw, the vet at the penitentiary."

I said, "They can afford to have a vet on the staff?"

He laughed, "Naw, he's an inmate."

"Bullshit."

He shook his head, "I ain't shitting you."

I said, "What's he in for?"

"Murder."

"A vet?"

"Yeah, killed his old lady and her lover."

I noticed the Pinal Mountains off in the east. They

loomed closer than I thought they should be. The way the sun backlit the mountains made lines of trees seem like I could reach out and get ahold of one.

He went on. "Yep, the State would have executed him if he hadn't been drunk when he killed them."

I said, "What difference does that make?"

"He'd been at the bar that night. When he came home she was getting it on with one of his best friends on the front room couch. It wasn't pre-meditated, I guess."

I said, "I guess."

You could see the penitentiary for miles before you got to it. Its solid gray walls jutted off the desert floor.

I wondered if Mimi was up drinking coffee out on the patio yet, watching the rising sun's ascent over the Aleppo pines in the backyards across the alley. Naw, I thought, she won't be up yet. The kids will be eating cold pizza and watching cartoons on the couch—she won't be up for hours—not the way she smelled of all those cigarettes— made me wish I hadn't partied so hard the day before— with frying and slicing all those bull nuts—felt like it might be all my fault.

As we pulled up to the main gate he said, "He'll be there when we're inseminating the cows."

I said, "Who?"

"That vet. Or ex-vet, I guess I should say. He lost his license to practice when they locked his ass up."

The guards at the main gate expected us because they waved us on through without forcing Darnell to stop. I figured they'd need to frisk us for weapons, drugs or what-ever.

I said, "Is Mr. Ex-vet the boss? Of us, I mean?"

"No, I'm the boss." He pointed to his chest and looked at me when he said that. The cigar stuck out of his mouth like a torpedo when he looked at me, his eyes emphatic. "He's there because that's his job in the prison. He takes care of the farm animals. We'll have a couple of trustees, too, to move the cows around the corrals and the alleys into the chute."

Instead of driving up to the penitentiary itself, we turned off towards a set of corrals about a half a mile away.

Darnell continued, "Webb's a pretty good guy. That's his name, Webb."

Between us and the dusty corrals, small tracts of ir-rigated land were planted in different crops. Most of the plots looked like cotton, but I also recognized wheat that needed combining in about a month, the bearded heads just turning from green to gold. Some small plots dotted with yellow safflower blooms and several fields of alfalfa calicoed in between the cotton and wheat fields. The alfalfa plots looked way past their primo harvest time—too many purple blooms spread across the green—loaded with honey bees hovering over the fields.

Darnell said, "Old Webb was the vet up in Holbrook. I imagine he took care of everything—range cattle, remuda horses and dog and cats besides—you know, a general practitioner of sorts."

Out in the fields twenty or so blue-shirted convicts chopped weeds in the cotton fields, a couple more moving irrigation hoses. Three khaki-clad prison guards mounted on horses rode around watching the men work. Long whips hung off the guards' saddle horns along with lassos.

Darnell continued, "I imagine he'll be a big help to us. He knows a lot about cattle."

As we pulled up to the corrals, I said, "Okay."

He stopped the truck and I started to get out. He grabbed my arm and pulled me across the seat and whis-pered, "Hey, don't say nothing to him about him killing those people."

A sudden urge to tell Darnell to kiss my ass for even thinking I'd be so damned stupid instantly penetrated my thoughts, but I refrained, just nodded.

Two Chicanos in blue work dungarees perched like blue

jays on one of the top horizontal-running sideboards of an alley that led from a large corral to a chute. The sides of the chute were about five feet tall and just wide enough for a cow to get through.

We stepped out of the pickup and Darnell strode around to the back and slid back the metal cover of his truck bed and nodded at a tank of frozen semen. "Put that under that tarp over there."

A small tarp stretched between three treated cedar posts made from old trestle ties that looked seasoned and smooth, their corners worn off. Reminded me of guided missiles waiting to go off. I recognized the sound of hoes chopping weeds in the cotton patches between us and the penitentiary and the sound of a horse snorting, too. Probably belonged to one of those guards.

The weight of the semen container surprised me, took both of my hands on the handles to pick it up and carry it. When I walked under the tarp and set the can down, I saw a large, raw-boned man sitting in the chute. He wore the same blue dungarees as the Chicanos sitting on the top sideboards of the alley.

He nodded and smiled, his mouth full of stained brown teeth. They reminded me of pictures of my father when young, before they pulled all his teeth out. My father used to call them water stains. I always thought of them as Okie stains. I wondered if this guy was some kind of Okie.

Darnell walked up and grinned when he noticed the man. He said, "Hey, Webb."

When Webb rose he didn't grab the chute's sideboards or posts or anything, he just rose and sauntered towards us with his large right hand stuck out to shake. Darnell looked down at his own hands and all the stuff he was carrying—pipettes, latex gloves, paper towels, a jug of water, and the coffee thermos—and gave Webb a stupid "how am I supposed to shake hands" look. Webb nodded one of those, "Yeah, I got you," looks.

Darnell motioned his head at me and said, "Webb, meet Marvin."

Again, the stained teeth. I nodded and shook his hand. Even though he didn't grip hard I could feel the power in that hand. I wondered if he choked her. With the power in those forearms and hands it would have been easy.

Darnell said, "Let's get to it."

Webb said, "Yep."

Darnell got the cattle prods and the whip out of the truck cab and gave them to the Chicanos. Webb hollered at them in Mexican and they jumped down from the top of the alley and ran off conversing in their rapid-fire lingo and pretty soon there were large black-and-white cows in the chute. From the length of their tails the cows appeared mature—broad-backed with bones jutting out all over.

I pulled on thin latex gloves. Darnell opened the can of semen and pulled a dose out and looked at me as vapor from the liquid nitrogen wafted into the air. He nodded. "Remember, Marvin, that shit would freeze your pecker in less that a second. You stick your hand in there it will shatter."

I flipped him a latex-covered, cream-colored middle finger as I smirked.

"Just need to be careful, hunh, Webb?"

Webb smiled. "Be careful."

Darnell looked at me, "You know how to preg test?"

I nodded and he chuckled, "You're the brand new A. I. certified technician so stick your hand up her ass and check her out, then I'll load the pipette with the semen and you can nail her."

I squirted lubricant on the glove of my left hand. The lubricant also acted as a disinfectant-like soap and I noticed its pungent odor as I stuck my hand into the first cow's ass. Right away it was a fight. She didn't like it and kicked at me through the slats and I imagined how that might feel if she got me in the nuts. Some shit shot out of her ass and got on my face. Darnell laughed and nodded at Webb.

I'd kind of lied about knowing how to test. In my college class, the teacher instructed us about three ways to pregnancy test cows but I only knew one way and that was to palpate a vein in there and if it pulsed like somebody was pumping lots of blood through a thin hose, then she was pregnant. I failed to master the other ways and lied to the instructor when I'd taken that part of the artificial insemination test at the junior college. I lied because I couldn't let Mimi think I failed.

Darnell said to Webb, "How's the general health of the herd? You need any vaccine or antibiotics? I got some in my pickup."

If Webb answered, I didn't hear it.

I found what I thought was the proper blood vessel. It wasn't pulsing. "She ain't knocked up."

Webb called out, "Why would she be?"

I said, "Maybe a stray bull snuck in and bred her one night."

Then it struck me, he might not like that. Might remind him of the stray that ended up in bed with his wife. He stared at me and neglected to show those stained teeth.

I added, "You know how bulls ..."

Darnell cut me off by clearing his throat and shooting a mouthful of spit on the dusty ground. "Give her a squirt," and handed me a pipette. I grabbed it in my right hand and stuck it between my teeth.

The pipette was wrapped in a paper towel so the direct heat of the sun wouldn't kill the semen drawn up inside. I could taste the white paper on my tongue. I groped around with my left hand inside her ass. I felt the cow's cervix through the thin wall of flesh that separated her reproductive tract from her waste elimination tract. The cervix seemed crooked and bent like it had been busted in half as Darnell said it might be. I wondered if Mimi's was like that. Not like the young cows we'd worked on in the class. This cow had thrown a lot of calves.

I finally found the uterus. I grabbed the pipette out of my mouth with my right hand and inserted the business end into the vagina. Using my left hand to feel the end of the pipette, I poked and fished around until I felt the business end slip out the back end of the cervix into the uterus. I squeezed the bulb on the end of the pipette and shot the semen inside.

I hoped I'd inseminated her as I smiled at Darnell and pulled my left hand out of her ass.

He said, "Don't get too happy. We only got fifty-nine more."

The arm I'd pushed up her ass already felt like it had been through my grandma's washing machine wringer. I understood why Webb and Darnell both owned big strong hands.

The morning heated up and I felt the hatband inside that new red hat soak with my sweat. I heard the Mexicans pop that whip on the backs of the cows and the hum of the electric prods as they jabbed cows in the flanks and the ribs, around the udders. For better than two hours I groped and flubbed around and I was still only half-way through. Darnell and Webb sat under the tarp palavering about cattle genetics and breeding and stuff like that.

Darnell yelled, "How you doing?" I didn't answer.

Then he yelled, "Better hurry it up, I need to go home and take a nap so I can go take my old lady out dancing tonight."

I blew sweat off my upper lip.

Besides me, the only other people working were the Mexicans inside the cattle pens pushing the cows into the chute so I could inseminate them, and the convicts out there in the cotton patches.

I rationalized having to do all the work by telling myself that to be good at breeding took a lot of practice.

Webb was saying, "I'd rather have a bull or two in here."
Darnell said, "Why?"
"I think the insemination takes better."

"Really?"

"Yeah, you technicians show up and who knows, maybe you hit the jackpot, maybe not. Then you leave, and it's like you were never here. A bull, now we know he's around— we see him and hear him and he instinctively knows what he's doing."

Darnell said, "Maybe."

Webb added, "The old ways are the best ways. No doubt about it after a bull mounts one of these cows."

I thought my left arm would fall off and right at that moment wished they had bulls at the prison, and then one of the cows kicked me, her foot cracking the tops and bottoms of the sideways slats meant to protect me. When her hard hoof bit into the skin over my shin bone, for at least four or five minutes I thought I'd pass out, but I knew I'd put up with a bunch of shit from Darnell so I just kept on groping, probing and squirting, trying to stand on one leg as I proceeded.

Webb liked to smoke a lot and kept firing up his Old Golds. The smell of his cigarettes burned the inside of my nose—reminded me of Mimi's big hair. I wondered what she was doing, if she was even up yet drinking her weak black coffee, reading the women's section of the local newspaper, the gossip column, who went to whose soiree.

The hack and click of the weed-chopping convicts in the cotton patches got louder and I wondered if they were getting closer. I could only spy the tops of the guards lounging on the backs of their mounts out there in the cotton patches. Must have been a change in the wind carrying the sound. Again the scent of Webb's cigarette smoke and again the image of Mimi sneaking into our bed. Did she or didn't she, and if she did and I caught her, could I act like we were only cats or dogs?

The cow I currently worked on suddenly pulled away, jerking me into the slats. I thought she'd yank my arm off. I yelled at the Mexicans to jab her with those electric prods and push her back up against the slats. When they did the cow bellowed and lifted her head back and rolled her big white eyeballs, then moved back against the slats.

I wondered how Webb felt when he stumbled into the house and interrupted his old lady and his best friend locked up in orgasm.

I found the cow's cervix and then I tried to work the pipette through the gristle-lined passageway to the uterus.

Did he go into a rage right away—did he even recognize what the hell was happening at first?

Sweat ran down my forehead and got in my right eye and burned as I squeezed a shot of semen in.

Did he watch them for a while before he killed them—a smile of satisfaction?

Over in the cotton patches men screamed at each other, some of it sounded like Mexican. I couldn't tell what was going on, but I heard a guard yell, "Cut out the fucking around."

Darnell said, "Let's take a break."

I walked over, slumped up against the side of the chute beneath the tarp and slipped down on my ass. I could feel cedar slivers go through my shirt and bury themselves in my back, but I was so tired I didn't care. I let out a big sigh.

Darnell said, "You alright?"

I nodded. Sweat burned my eyes. My arms felt like they'd been crushed in a vice.

He said, "Cat got your tongue?'

I shook my head, no.

He said, "Worried about your old lady?"

He grinned and said to Webb, 'Him and his old lady are having it out."

I yanked my head around and frowned at him. I blurted, "I love her."

Webb nodded his head and lit up an Old Gold.

Darnell smiled at me, "You want a sandwich?"

I nodded and Webb said, "No."

Darnell walked off to get the ice chest with the grub in it. I looked at Webb who stared at the ground and I imagined him wrapping his hands around his wife's neck after he killed the friend. The thunder of horse hooves and a lot of yelling from the cotton patch carried over our direction. I couldn't make out what all the fuss was about.

I wondered how he felt as he placed his callused thumbs on her throat and slowly started to squeeze. A whip snapped in the distance, then somebody screamed. Webb looked in the direction of the convicts working in the fields. His hard eyes owned a pinpoint energy that burned through the air. I wondered if he wore that look as she kicked and screamed and begged him not to kill her, tears streaming down her cheeks. Or did tears stream down his cheeks, or did he have an orgasm maybe, squirting all over the inside of his white cotton briefs?

I said, "How'd it feel?"

He turned those eyes on me and burned me. Somewhere out there in the cotton patches the sound of the whip snapped again and again. Webb wasn't showing any of those stained teeth. Somebody screamed.

Heezey's Wake

Heezey caught a dose of cancer. She fought like hell. Took chemo, drank contraband herbs smuggled from Mexico, lost her hair. She patched the best face on it. At the Halloween party she used the sprouting roots of hair on her head as part of her costume, a white-faced ghoul like you used to see at the Saturday double features.

Reality trumped pluck and she got cancer again. Ate her up. Like a rattlesnake you see on one of those nature shows; a frog or rabbit half swallowed, legs scrabbling frantic-like. She quit on a Sunday afternoon when a dust storm flayed the paint off Cadillacs. Wednesday she was in the ground.

Me and her old man, Hooter, went back to the cemetery that Wednesday night and saw herds of rabbits hopping around the gravestones. Big old jacks with their ears jabbing the air. Cottontails, too. Hoppy-hopping from one headstone to the next munching Bermuda grass.

Hooter and I'd slammed a few VOs and were all chewed up after hauling relatives from the airport, ones that hadn't been heard from in decades. Old ladies wearing way too much make-up, blue hair, thick-heeled shoes that needed polish.

At the cemetery we parked his Dodge and slumped low in the seats, watched the rabbits graze, headlights etching the black. We sucked on Buds.

Hooter said, "You know the bitch was cheating on me

before she got sick?"

I didn't answer.

He said, "Damned near blew her head off. And her fuckhead lover's, too."

Hooter looked out his side window.

He said, "Found them in a motel down on Washington. Where Tempe and Phoenix meet."

I started to ask how he found them, but let it ride.

He said, "I was parked right outside. Had both kids with me. They were so freaked out they looked like statues."

He swigged beer, sloshed it around, spit it out.

He said, "Right fucking there. I had them. My shotgun loaded, #1 shot, three-inch magnums."

I shook my head like I was impressed.

He said, "Would have done some splattering."

I said, "How come you didn't blow their asses away?"

He said, "Wasn't worth going to the pen. Some damned convict lifer riding my ass like a whore."

He stared at me. Tears spilled out.

He said, "Besides. You know. The kids."

I said, "Yeah."

He said, "And now it's just me and them."

I turned my head. Couldn't look him in the eye.

He said, "Look at them damned rabbits."

I swallowed some beer. It was warm, turned my stomach.

He slumped, sniffling and shivering.

The headlights cut the night like claws grasping at cobwebs. He started his engine and drove around the graveyard, light capturing the eyes of the rabbits as they hopped, a little frenzy, the way they held their ears. Not quite straight, but pointed off in the direction of the black.

He said, "Them damned rabbits are going to eat all the grass."

I said, "Hell no, not all. It's what keeps them alive."

He looked at me; his swollen eyelids, his streaked and ruddy face.

He said, "Look at them rabbits. They're all around Heezey's grave."

I couldn't have told you where Heezey's grave was. They all looked the same, the headstones dark grey, cut at predictable angles.

He said, "Pissing me off."

I watched the rabbits. They hopped a bit, nibbled some, looked around and listened with their long ears, nibbled, hopped some.

He said, "Fucking rabbits."

I looked north, to town. Its lights flitted like it was meandering.

He opened the car door and climbed out, left the door open. I heard the trunk. It croaked like an old toad. I watched him stride into the headlights. He was carrying a sawed-off ax handle. It was familiar to me. A leather thong strung through a hole drilled in the end. So you could grip it. Good for busting heads. Painted black. Cored out and filled with lead. It was familiar. Made it myself. Gave it to him for Christmas one year. Good for busting heads.

The rabbits didn't seem to care. They kept nibbling and hopping. He slumped into a stalk; a small cottontail. Hooter swung, missed, then started to flail. I saw flying cottontail. Then a jack with his ears knocked down and bloody. The rabbits reminded me of sheep when a coyote gets in their midst. Frightened. Run a little ways, stop and look, gang up, eyes catching starlight, red reflection like being caught in a bad photograph.

Hooter swung the sawed-off ax handle. There was blood on his white shirt.

He screamed, "Heezey."

His smooth-soled boots slipped on the grass. He stumbled. More than once. Slow motion. He swung. Headstones glittered. I thought I heard a voice; high keening.

Like Heezey might do. I didn't know rabbits could speak. I looked away. The lights of town. They seemed to be going somewhere.

The Sunday Dishes

We hugged. But it wasn't a hug of love. It was a truce hug. I squeezed hard but she was cold. Well, not cold, but not very responsive. It was like an open-pit garbage hole. The way my stomach felt.

She said, "Another bad night, huh?"

I said, "I don't know how many more I can take."

She pulled away and smiled, said, "You're young."

I said, "I don't feel like it."

I tried to hug her again, get closer, slip my leg in-between hers, but she pulled away and looked into my eyes. Today hers were very green and seemed at odds with her dark-black hair. I could feel my eyes start to dart. As if caught in a lie. I watched her eyes watching mine. Hers were scurrying, too. The way they darted reminded me of fast bass guitar playing in a fast rock and roll song. I looked down. She pulled away.

She said, "I need to go to the store."

I shot her a please-don't-go look.

She said, "You can do the breakfast dishes."

I said, "I need to go out, too. Who's going to watch the kids?"

She said, "Don't worry about that. They can watch themselves."

I felt like fast racehorses way behind the front-runner.

She went to the bathroom.

I thought about last night. She said she was just going for a ride. Had been doing a lot of that lately. Just going for

a ride. What the fuck was she doing just going for a ride?
At night. What the hell was she looking at? She kept telling
me that, that she was going out in the night just to look at
the night. Yeah, bullshit. Look at what? The stars? The stars
on a dust-filled night? The smut of the breezes capturing the pulverized soil of cotton ground being readied for
planting? What stars? I asked her that last week.

We were standing out in the night, arm-in-arm. Then I
looked at the sky and asked her if she knew the story of
Orion. I pointed him out overhead. His bright star belt, his
sword, his legs. She couldn't see it. Said she'd never heard
of Orion.

I told her about how he'd fallen in love with some Greek
goddess, the sister of Apollo or Adonis or some other deity.
How the brother wouldn't have that. Orion was a giant,
could walk across the seas, keep his head above water.
Apollo or Adonis, or whoever the hell wasn't liking Orion
loving his sister, shot Orion in the head with an arrow as
he was walking through some sea, the Aegean probably, or
maybe the Adriatic. Killed his ass dead. But Zeus took pity
on Orion, stuck him up in heaven so that everybody could
see him, know his sad tale.

After I had finished telling her that story she had looked
at me and laughed. I thought the myth was sad. She
laughed.

I couldn't get the idea of the stars and night out of my
mind. I wasn't getting the dishes clean. I knew it. Didn't
give a shit. Just kept seeing her car going down long
straight roads, every once in a while a stand of thick cottonwood on a dirt ditch bank, and the dirty sky and some
stars that meant nothing to her.

I could hear her in the bathroom, putting on her face.
Just to go to the store? The window over the sink was
smudged, needed cleaning. Time was, that wouldn't have
been necessary. But now, who knows?

Outside the window, a large mulberry tree was sprouting new leaves. The green was exuberant. I looked at the lower right windowpane and then looked at my hands in the dishwater, at the scar on the back of my right hand. Light refracted through soapy water, made the scar stand out. It looked red and angry. I remembered the day I got it. Lost a bet on a football game. Fucking Dallas Cowboys. Now I never bet against them.

At the time she'd laughed at me. I told her I needed money to pay for my lost bet. She'd told me to go to hell. I'd made the stupid bet, I could find the money some-place else. I stuck my fist through the windowpane. She'd stopped laughing.

I kept looking at the windowpane as I put the dishes away. It hadn't been put back in correctly. There was a crack in the corner. My handiwork again.

She came out of the bathroom and grabbed her purse, started for the door. I grabbed her and hugged. She was stone cold.

I said, "Sorry about last night."

She almost grinned.

I said, "I can't stand many more like that."

She relaxed and hugged back. Just a little.

I said, "Don't be long."

She stiffened, said, "I told you to stop telling me what to do."

I said, "I thought maybe we could have a nice afternoon, the kids and us, you know?"

Her eyes weren't as green as before. I could see little flecks of red. Reminded me of the night before. How I shattered the vase, sent red roses across the floor. She'd brought them home from work. Said she'd been given them for doing some special job. I asked her out loud what job that might be. She didn't like that.

I looked past her and shook my head, said, "No more nights like that. Too much anger. And no sleep. Almost as bad as my time in the war."

She snorted.

I said, "What the hell's that mean?"

She said, "You and your war. It's always about your war. Like the rest of us haven't had shit happen to us."

I said, "Not like mine."

She smirked and pulled away, said, "After I get done at the grocery store, I think I'll go for a ride."

Caesar

Amaro showed up outside my house. I watched him through the picture window. He parked between my date palm and my California fan palm. A Mexican kid sat on the wheel well in the back of the pickup. He looked thirteen, maybe fourteen years old.

I watched Amaro amble up to the front steps, where he turned and yelled something in Spanish. The kid gave him a slight nod and then sat on his hands as Amaro rang my doorbell. I let him ring it twice and then, just for orneriness, I let him pick up the heavy brass knocker and drop it, once, twice, three times, before I walked over and opened the door.

He grinned at me like he owned some new gossip. He stuck his fist out and said, "*Ora le, cuñado.*"

I bumped his fist with mine and said, "Hey, brother-in-law, what do you want?"

He grinned again and then let out a little burst of laughter. The stench of digested beer hit me and I scrunched up my nose. He said, "Fuck you."

"Yes, very much."

His gold-capped teeth shone from the light in the ceiling of my foyer. "I got a new son."

"I didn't know Mercy was pregnant. As much as I see her, you'd think I'd have noticed her being heavy with a kid."

He frowned and flicked his head like what I'd said was some big bother. "You're always so fucking sarcastic. You know she wasn't pregnant."

"Yes, I am fucking sarcastic and yes, I know she was not pregnant because I saw her yesterday at the western store when I went in to get me a new pair of boots."

He put his arms out and shrugged like everything in the world was just plain elementary and why was I giving him such a hard time about everything.

I nodded. "Tell me about your new son."

He grinned again and sidled around, kind of like my Queensland blue heeler does when you go to pet him. "You got any beer?"

"Don't you think it's a little early, and besides, from the smell of your bad breath, you've already been at it."

His eyes got big. "You can tell?"

"I can tell." I glared at him, then chuckled, "Okay, and as you like to say, 'Anytime is beer time.'"

I motioned him into the house and nodded, "Make sure all the sheep shit's off your boots or your sister will be all over my ass, and yours."

"Fuck her." He leaned against the wall and checked the bottoms of both boots.

I said, "No. That's my job."

"What is?"

I said it real loud. "To fuck her."

He laughed as we moved through the living room into the kitchen. He prissed around like a caricature of the feminine and hissed, "Don't you mean, make love?"

I yelled, "All those things."

He yelled back. "It's your fucking duty, ain't it?"

As I pulled two bottles of Coors out of the fridge, I yelled louder, "It's my duty to service the womenfolk."

"Just don't service Mercy."

When he yelled that it sounded like he was pissed off and yes, I would service Mercy, if given the opportunity, but I didn't think she'd let me. And besides, just as well, what with all the family ties.

I sat at the big round table in the dining room and said, "Just not Mercy."

He sat down and using my beer opener popped the top off his bottle and took a long deep drink. He sighed when he swallowed.

I pointed towards the front of the house, "You going to leave that Mexican kid out in the back of the truck?"

He said, "That's my new son."

I must have worn a really stupid look because he pointed at me and started to give me one of his really goofy giggles that sound like three or four girls at a slumber party talking about letting boys do it to them.

I got control of my facial expressions. "What's your new son's name?"

"*César.*"

When he said the name it was like he was yelling at me because he was pissed off. "You mean his name is Caesar—like the Roman kings."

He barked at me. "No. *César.* It's like this, 'say-czar,' like *César* the Mexican kid from Rillito. 'Cause that's where he's from, lately anyway."

"How come you say it with all that violence?"

"Because I like how it sounds coming out of my mouth." He stuck his thumbs under the collar of his Levi shirt and said, "I am violent. I am one bad fuck."

That made me laugh because it's true and everyone knows it but everyone is afraid to say it, so he says it himself. All the time.

I nodded. "From Rillito, hunh? Only thing down there is cotton camps, bars and whorehouses."

He didn't respond, just took a suck off the end of his bottle of Coors.

I leaned forward over the table. "Who's his mama?"

"Perdita Flores."

"Is she a whore?"

He shook his head. "Naw."

When he said that he looked me straight in the eye. Not lying, I thought. Well, maybe, I thought. Sometimes Amaro lies and it looks like he's telling the truth.

I licked my mustache. The cuckoo clock in the living room sang out eight o'clock.

"Don't you think we ought to ask him in?"

"Naw. It'll do him good to sit out there."

I scratched the knuckles of my left hand. "What do you need another kid for?"

"Aw, he can help me out around the feedlot. We can be buddies."

I shook my head. "But you've already got two sons with your first two wives, and three daughters, too. And that doesn't count the ones out of wedlock, the ones we don't know about."

He waved his thick fist in front of my face. "Fuck them."

"What does Mercy think about *César*?"

"Aw, she likes it. He can clean the house."

I stood up and looked out the window of the den. I could hear my heeler over by the gate that led out into the front yard. He barked and snarled like there was an intruder outside. Amaro belched. Caesar wasn't in the back of the truck. I moved around so I could see up and down the street, around the front yard. No sign of Caesar. I wondered where he'd escaped to. I had a clear view to the south and didn't see anything except old man Patterson's tan stucco house and what remained of his orange grove. A big red bougainvillea at my next door neighbor's blocked my view of the north, but I just knew he was gone—hightailed it away from Amaro. And just as well. The kid wouldn't do anything to please Mercy. She'd be bitching and whining about rings in the toilet bowl and hardened food on the supposedly clean dishes and Caesar'd be wondering why the hell she was bitching when she had it so good. And she'd stick those perky knockers of hers out like some kind of national anthem and then she'd start to sniffle and

Amaro would knock the kid around, bust his lip, bruise him some, and then Caesar would have to get on his knees and scrub the vinyl floors and Mercy would let Amaro lick her nipples and do whatever he wanted.

Amaro yelled at me. "*Cuñado*, what's up out there?"

"Nothing," I said. "Absolutely nothing."

Top and Bottom

I had my eggs over-easy and hash browns and slab of over-cooked ham and now I sat out on the covered boardwalk on a rough-hewn white pine bench and watched the cars slide sideways on the ice down Top and Bottom Street.

Clumps of cumulus hurried from the west and the wind got caught in the tops of the ponderosas and made the giant trees sway. Their sound filled the morning with a hint of storm.

Across the street, gobs of snow splattered the City National Bank's blue paint job and faux rock façade. Earlier, the village snowplow cleaned off the streets and piled an icy berm that blocked access to the bank's drive-through, so the German lady who ran the bank was out there in her dress and moon boots trying to clear a path.

As I looked at her I tried to imagine what she might be like to make love to, but she was old. I got a vision of a lot of wrinkles around her privates and besides, she was a fucking Nazi.

Down yonder below the vacant lot across from the bank, a blue 1965 Ford pickup slid into the Texaco and a thin Apache got out and walked into the service station's office. He wasn't in there long and when he came out he looked back and shot the finger at whoever was working in the station. Then he got back in his pickup and drove out from beneath the veranda that protected the gas pumps from bad weather. The truck rumbled and grunted. Sounded like it needed at least a new head gasket and maybe more. It also needed a new muffler. I figured the town Nazi-cop would put the siren and lights on him before he got much farther. They don't like a lot of noise in this town.

The woman who worked at the front desk in the forest service office across the highway to Artesia walked by me. Brownwood and I called her Old Good Looking. She wore a long purple coat, fringed with fake purple fur around the hood over her head. The color went just right with her pale face and her amber-colored eyes. She thought she was hot stuff, and to be frank, so did I. I smiled at her, but her being a Church-of-Christer, she didn't have much to do with me. Just before she got parallel with me I could see she had the top part of that fancy purple coat open and she had her suit jacket open too, and for Christ's sake, she had the top two buttons on her lavender tinted blouse open, too. I saw her cleavage. She nabbed me staring at that spot and I swear by God her skin turned red. I sniggered.

Right then Brownwood's old lady appeared from the frozen north-facing road that ran up the hill to her house. Contrary to her usual driving style, the black Chevy Suburban crept through the intersection and toward Top and Bottom Street and turned into the service station.
I decided to sit a spell until I was sure the post office folks had the mail in the boxes before I went down there.

The Indian I had seen over at the Texaco drove up to the bank and went inside, and I thought good luck in there with all them Jesus-fearing Church-of-Christer hick Nazis and I was right because he quickly came out. He said something I couldn't understand and then kicked a chunk of old ice plowed up and packed in the berm by the snowplow. I could see he wore a Levi shirt and no coat and he also wore pointy-toe riding boots. I wondered how he kept from getting cold. I wondered how he kept from falling on his ass in those boots without some kind of waffle tread to give him some traction.

He crossed the street and went into the bar, but I knew what that would get him. Nazis again; Nazis don't like anybody but white people. Everybody from the Arizona border to south Texas knew how that old Nazi bag that kept the bar felt about "them goddamned Indians."

Brownwood's old lady drove up Top and Bottom. Seemed like she was aimed right at me. She turned right and stared at me as she drove towards the post office. It looked like she was smiling. She parked across the street from the post office in a no-parking zone and went in to do some mail business.

And sure enough, right on cue, a ruckus got up inside the bar and I chuckled as I got up and walked down to the post office to get my mail feeling some pity for that damned Apache.

Brownwood's old lady came out with a handful of envelopes and instead of crossing the street to her Suburban, she stopped and stared at me as I walked along. I thought about turning around so I didn't have to face her, but I didn't want anybody to think I was weak.

I stopped to consider my options and as I did, Old Good Looking who worked in the forest service office walked towards me. She looked at me and I looked back and right then I noticed that smoky gaze a woman gives you when she's thinking the same thing you are thinking. My main chance, I thought. She's thinking about it, I thought, about me. It felt like a lizard scrabbled all around the insides of my thighs. I ought to ask her to supper, I thought, but I didn't.

I said, "Morning." The rouge on her face and the makeup on her eyelids went with the purple coat.

She gave me a brief nod and walked on. I liked the fact that she wore high heels out in this weather with all the ice and snow. Gutsy broad, I thought. I wondered what she would look like, what she'd be like, underneath the red and white Navajo blanket my mother gave me for Christmas.

I thought, I ought to call her tonight. She'd given me that look. That's when you know you have to move. That's when the woman is wondering what you and she might be like. Not just someone to shoot the shit with, but more intimate things.

Brownwood's old lady stood in front of the post office and watched all this take place. She sneered and hissed something to Old Good Looking who shot something back. As Old Good Looking went into the post office, Brownwood's old lady gave her the finger. Then she turned her gaze on me and moved in my direction. She wore waffle stompers and showed no fear that she might step on a patch of ice and bust her ass either. By then I wasn't so sure she was smiling and suddenly felt like I had an Indian renegade aiming arrows at my back.

When she came close she shot me a wicked little sneer as she held those envelopes in her left hand and ran the ends back and forth over the flat of her right palm. The ratcheting sound made me feel like I was full of scrabbling scorpions.

She said, "Wondering what she'll look like beneath that classy Navajo blanket on your bed?"

I know my face turned red. I felt it, and knowing that it was turning red made me cringe.

I didn't answer her so she grinned and said, "People just won't admit it. It's all about sex. You look at a woman, you wonder what she'd be like in bed."

She tapped her right toe on the concrete and the sun got in my eyes and made me tear up.

She giggled and said, "When I look at a man I wonder what he'd be like in bed. It's all about sex."

Right then her eyes looked like cat's eyes—a tawny yellow. I looked at her fingernails as she scratched the side of her neck. She wore a bold shade of purple polish—a regal purple. I quickly glanced at where I thought Old Good Looking might be behind that glass in the post office window, but the sun's glare blinded me.

Brownwood's old lady smirked, "And the thought of strange pussy has the biggest yank of all."

I know my eyes bugged out on my face and I stuttered, "But she's a ... she's a Church-of-Christer."

She laughed, "You're so naive."

She looked at the Apache as he drove up and parked in front of the post office. He got out and asked someone for a loan. Brownwood's old lady stared at him for a few seconds and then turned to me. "It's so sad."

I shrugged and said, "What's so sad?"

She stuck her tongue out at me as she waived me off. As she turned she muttered something like, "Don't waste your words."

I headed for the post office door and then she yelled, "Hey."

Reluctant to turn towards her I yelled back, "What?"

"You get my cash?"

"I gave it to Brownwood."

"What did you say?"

I imagined what everybody thought about us standing out there yelling.

"I gave it to Brownwood."

A lot of people crowded around the front counter shooting the shit with Nicolette who was the second-in-command at the post office. She towered over them as they all leaned on the counter and talked about I don't know what. Old Good Looking in the long purple coat stood in the crowd, so I supposed it might have been talk about God. I walked over and waved at Nicolette and as I did I got as close as propriety allowed so I could admire Old Good Looking's cleavage again. As I leered at her she blushed. I imagined my tongue circling one of her nipples and then nipping at it when it got stiff and covered with goosebumps.

I glanced out the window to see if Brownwood's old lady was still outside. She wasn't, but just the same, I tried to imagine me licking her aureoles, too, but I failed to get any charge out of that.

I went to Box 1249 and got my Sears throw-outs and as I turned, that Indian came through the door. He had a look on his face that made me wonder if he hadn't been stabbed in the back. I chuckled to think of the battle he'd fought with that fucking Nazi in the bar.

The Apache headed for Nicolette and Old Good Looking and all the other people palavering over there by the counter. I got a shot of his profile. He had a pug nose and seemed younger than I originally thought. He needed a haircut. His black hair hung in a thick braid down past the tops of his shoulders. I hadn't noticed earlier, but his shirt was embroidered denim with figures of hawks and fish and bears all over the yoke on both the front and the back. His boots had silver tips on their points and besides their obvious age, were polished to a high shine that deflected beads of melted ice that had accumulated on the decorative stitching on the vamp. He had a big silver and turquoise ring on his right ring finger and his wristwatch sported a silver band that must have weighed better than a pound.

I thought to myself, he's a walking bank vault with all that silver on, and what with the price of silver these days ... that was before I noticed his thin squash blossom. That didn't look Apache, but more like something a Zuni would make, but still, even as far away as he was, I could tell by the work that it was worth a ton.

I looked at Old Good Looking who was looking at me and then she turned her head quick like she hadn't been looking at me. The way her hair swayed made me think of Brownwood's old lady and how she hurt my feelings with the way she acted outside.

I heard them shooting the shit around the post office countertop as the Apache's boots thumped on the vinyl floor. I heard him say, "I'm about out of gas and I need to get back to my house on the reservation. Could you spare some change? Anything?"

Nobody said a thing.

I heard him walk away and he entered my view as I sorted through my junk mail at a little table against the wall. The preacher from the Church of Christ came in and ignored that Indian like he wasn't alive. And the old man that owned the Chuck Wagon Restaurant that gave singing dinners in the summer … him, too. To be fair, at least he said something. I didn't hear what.

I pulled out my pocket watch and noticed it was time for me to go do something productive. Old Good Looking tried to sneak by that Indian but he accosted her anyway. She shook her head and moved back towards Nicolette's counter.

I walked up to the front door, staring at the back of his damp Levi shirt. I thought I saw him shiver. He stared off at the ladies who huddled around Nicolette with their backs turned so as not to have to watch him watch them.

I reached for the door handle hoping to get away before he caught me but he swung around and said, "Say, Mister, I'm out of gas and need to get back to the reservation. Could you give me some money?"

I didn't like the frank way his black eyes looked into mine. I started to shake my head.

He put his hand in his right front pocket and I suddenly shied back. I'd heard they liked knives. Big ones.

He didn't seem to care about my reservations. "Here, Mister. I'll give you this ring."

I looked down at the open palm of his hand and was surprised by the long, elegant fingers. Right in the middle of his open hand was a large silver and turquoise ring. The sun's glint hit the silver and it twinkled like the stars in the Milky Way over town at night.

I wanted to say, "Don't do this," but I didn't. I wanted to vamoose but I couldn't because the quality of the rock in that silver was fine, not the reformulated Iranian shit you get so much, faked and sold as the real Indian deal.

I looked back at his face and he smiled. His straight white teeth surprised me. And his face didn't have a lot of blackheads as I expected.

I thought, I hope he doesn't do this, as I ran my hand in my right front pocket looking for the keys to my Ford Bronco. I felt a bill and some change. I pulled it out and saw a five spot and some quarters and dimes. For some stupid fucking reason I shoved it at him.

"It's all I got."

He stared at me as he reached out and took the money. I thought I saw a tear in his eye.

He reached his open palm with the ring toward me and offered, "Thanks, Mister. Here."

"No, I don't want it."

He was crying. I felt my face get hot and I couldn't look at him. He left.

Old Good Looking walked up to me and said, "You are a really nice man."

I stared at her amber-colored irises, but there was no smoke, much less any fire in there. The light they reflected seemed weak. I wondered about catching a glimpse of her cleavage but my eyes refused to move. I noticed some of the purple threads of the quilting on her coat collar sticking up.

I turned and walked off as I heard the preacher say something to her. Out on Top and Bottom Street I heard him say something about Brownwood's old lady, too, but I didn't really catch the gist of it.

Pugilist

I noticed Juanita. She cleaned rooms in the motel next door. She toted black plastic bags of garbage, or armfuls of dirty white linen down the metal steps. She worked fast. When she skipped down the metal steps, the sound thrummed into the ponderosa pines growing on the hill behind.

I thumped upstairs to my place and when I walked in noticed the blinking red light on my answering machine.

My ex-wife Sassy's voice yelled at me, "I didn't get the child support check."

She paused but I knew more would come. "How am I supposed to feed these kids?"

Another pause, like she was waiting for me to answer. "Hello. Don't you care about your kids?"

Heartburn shot up my throat and I coughed.

Another long pause. "Send the fucking check."

I sat in the café with my back in the corner so I could watch the front door. Waiting for Carter to arrive. I dug into ground beef smothered with a red chili cheese sauce on an open-faced burger bun. A chipped white cup full of bitter coffee. Next to me, wearing his battered Stetson and brown canvas Carhartt, Rifton T. sliced chunks off a rare Porterhouse steak. Blood mixed with hot fat flowed across the white plate into a pile of French fries.

The first time I know I saw Juanita she drove up to the

motel in an old 1968 canary yellow Dodge Charger with
mud splattered all over the front and the sides. A white
bumper sticker with big red letters. "Indian Power." Someone must have ripped the sticker before it got stuck on
the bumper. The words "Indian Power" didn't quite fit
together.

As usual, Carter proved tardy. Outside, a cold spring rain
drizzled off the eaves over the boardwalk. The old wood
floor beneath us smelled of years of skunk and cigarette
smoke.

Juanita said, "I'm Navajo. Real Navajo. Not one of those
Anglicized or Mexicanized Navajos. I'm real." A big red
purse dangled off her left elbow. The same red as her
fingernail polish and her lipstick. Blood red and scary
because later I discovered a long-barreled Ruger .22 Mag
pistol in the bottom of that big red purse along with a
bunch of white mints and three one-hundred-dollar bills
folded and stashed in a silver and turquoise money clip
inlaid with a ram's head.
She wore boots with very high heels. Black boots, and
her prints were obvious in either mud or snow. Just like
her Dodge Charger snow tire tracks.
I first met her in a bar. I wore expensive jeans that
showed off my tight ass. And a checked black and white
cowboy shirt pegged in the back to show off my wide
shoulders and narrow waist. And a three-inch snap-brim
come-fuck-me Stetson silverbelly 5X beaver.
I felt her eyes on my back and I spotted her in the mirror. Her caramel colored skin. She wore a Stetson, too, the
crown not shaped with dips and dimples like the cowboys
do, but up like the end of a .45 caliber slug—like the Indians wore in John Wayne's movies. She sported long black
hair done up in braids. She kept looking at my ass. I caught
her reflection just over the tops of the Metaxa bottles and

the fancy Spanish brandies.

I turned and bored straight into her black eyes, held up my bottle of Coors and asked, "What'll you have?"

At the restaurant I saw Carter standing next to the potbelly stove. Rainwater leaked onto the top of the cast iron and sizzled. He kept his hands jammed in his pockets and palavered with a small Chicano wearing a red scarf around his neck like one of those movie stars in flicks you see from the 1930s. He had on a red beret. He wasn't a dark Chicano, but he was still a Chicano. I could tell by the way he talked. Used his hands a lot. Stuck his thumbs and little fingers out from clenched fists to punctuate something important. Shrugged his shoulders as he screwed up his pasty face. I imagined him using words like, "*homey*" and "*esse*" and "*vato.*"

Juanita played hard-to-get. I followed her through a blizzard to a party. Someone supposedly scratched some lines. I didn't find them. The party proved too mellow for me. I told her to come home with me and I'd show her what I owned. She smiled, then lifted a slender right index finger and wagged a no-way signal.

I liked the way her braids swayed when she moved. She had good knockers for a small woman. I didn't like the look of her nose. Too big.

A couple of nights later I found her in a saloon drinking Perrier with a bunch of the fucked-up locals. I managed to squeeze onto the stool next to her. We chatted about Navajos and tribal stuff and the way the weather warmed and how the banks of snow disappeared in the teeth of the Chinook that blew in from the west and sucked up all the moisture.

She laughed at me and ran her fingers across my cheek and said, "See. See how dry the Chinook has made my fingertips?"

They didn't feel dry to me. I shivered and knew I had my chance.

I said, "Let's go for a ride."

She smiled and nodded.

In my Ford Bronco she couldn't get close because of the goddamned captain's seats. I said, "Where to?"

She said, "I can't go for a ride. Take me to where I'm staying."

It had suddenly turned colder. The rain froze to the telephone wires. I thought about dropping her off in the street. "Where's that?"

She giggled. "Don't sound so disappointed. I have to go check on my daughter."

I looked out the window on my side. The hulks of spruce trees choked the freezing streets.

We drove to a part of town I'd never been to. The poor part of town. We stopped in front of a house with weathered cedar shingles beneath a bright streetlight. Two ancient Dodge Power Wagons loaded with piñon rounds that needed splitting were parked in front of the house. A wood splitter sat next to a beat-up fence beside at least six cords of wood.

She started to get out. I grabbed her hand. "Can I come in?"

She grinned. I liked the way the light shone on her teeth. "Everybody in there has the flu."

"I don't get the flu."

"Oh, heap big white man."

I laughed.

Inside I smelled the remnants of fried pork and collard greens. Empty Coors bottles littered the kitchen table.

She squeezed my hand and whispered, "Shh, I'll be right back."

Snow pack boots lined the wall. A big snow shovel leaned against the back door. A Dallas Cowboys poster hung on the wall along with some paintings of local landscapes. I walked up close to the wall to get a better glimpse of those paintings and tripped over a sleeping Dachshund.

It yipped and trotted off into a dark room. A lot of the
paintings were of falling-down barns and cabins in drifts of
snow and sheets of summer rain. The fir trees looked real.
There was a portrait of a red roan stallion that showed
some skill, the legs the right shape and proportion. The
withers, too. Some paintings of aspens looked too grim.
Something about the way the black knuckles where the
limbs had fallen off seemed to not really fit on the trunks
of the trees.

I heard Juanita and I nodded at the paintings. "Who lives
here?"

She grabbed my hand and gave her head a quick shake.
"Let's go back out."

In the Bronco she let me kiss her. My tongue slipped
right in. I tried to touch her intimates but she grabbed my
fingers and squeezed. "I'm going to San Francisco tomorrow afternoon."

I didn't give a shit where she was going. I tried to kiss
her again, but she turned her face towards the car window.

I sat back and sighed. "That's a long way from here."

"Yeah, but there are lots of Indins there."

I liked how she said Indins for Indians.

I leaned over and pulled her face close and tried to kiss
her again.

She said, "I don't want you to get sick."

I sighed and we kissed.

She said, "I got to go. Come see me in San Francisco."

I thought, why in the hell would I go to San Francisco?
I took my wallet out and found a piece of paper folded in
there. There was a phone number for a real estate agent
who had fucked me when she thought I might buy a house
from her. I handed the "Indin" the paper and said, "How
can I get in touch with you?"

I handed her a pen and she wrote on the paper.

Large drops of rain mixed with sleet slapped on my
windshield. She handed me back the paper.

It said Georgette Billy and a phone number.

She said, "That's my cousin. She lives right in San Francisco."

She grabbed both of my hands and squeezed and pulled me close and kissed me dead on the lips and then got out.

She said, "Come see me."

She ran in her high-heeled boots through sheets of freezing rain.

Next to the steamy woodstove, Carter pulled his hat off and ran his fingers through his hair. Rifton T. cut a thick piece of juicy steak and jammed it into his mouth. He used the point of his knife. Carter grabbed the Chicano's arm and led him in our direction. Rifton T. looked up and said, "Well lookee there, old Tommy Carmona, ex-con."

I cleared my throat, balled my fists and glanced at the front door to the café. Besides his red beret and red scarf around his neck, this Carmona guy wore a short-sleeved khaki shirt. I wondered if he had goosebumps on his naked arms.

Rifton T. mumbled while chewing a long French fry, "Hell of a boxer, hell of a boxer."

The Chicano sported khaki trousers and a wide black belt with a huge silver buckle in the shape of a square. I thought I saw the outside edge of the buckle glint in the overhead lamps. I rubbed the palms of my hands on my Levis to wipe the sweat off. I'd heard convicts sharpened belt buckles in the pen. Used them as weapons.

Carter seemed ecstatic as he drew near. "Rifton, Rifton, look who's here."

On his feet Carmona wore heavy black brogans with numerous wrinkles, the paint worn off the eyelets. I tried to inspect his hands.

Rifton T. grumbled while gnawing a chunk of bloody steak. "I see him, Carter. I see him."

Muscles bulged on the shut-your-fucking-mouth backs

of Carmona's hands. Colored like old paste, the palms puffed up between the lifeline, the heart line, the head line and the circle of Venus. He jammed his right hand between Rifton T.'s face and his steak. "Gimmee five."

I thought I caught him glancing at me.

I flunked out of college my freshman year. So I don't remember much they told me there. My least favorite course was anthropology. Useless information—won't tell you anything about cycling cows, or how to change out the blades of a sickle so you can cut hay.

The professor was a woman who looked like a man. She acted like a man, too. One thing she told me in class stuck, though. Glabrous. That's when a woman doesn't have any hair on her body. Check that, they may have hair on their head, but not on the rest of them.

My "Indin" friend didn't leave when she said. She found me in the bar. Me and some of the local wood-butchers stomped on the floor to piss the skunks off. The place smelled bad. My "Indin" friend had mud on her high-heeled boots and on her jeans like she'd been jumping up and down outside in the dirt road. Her Stetson was wet. Her black hair hung free of her braids. It dangled down to the top of her butt. It was thick and shone in the gaslights hanging on the back bar. I laughed, "You need a bath."

She grinned.

I ran upstairs before the "Indin" got out of my Bronco so I could make sure I didn't have any nasty messages from Sassy on the answering machine.

She was glabrous. Her legs the smoothest I'd ever touched. And other places.

As I watched *Red River* on the late night TV movie, she stood in the doorway of my bathroom with a brown bath towel around her. She was small. The towel went from just above her knockers to just above her knees. She had small feet.

She said, "This Indin girl loves your towels."

I replied, "That's really something to love." I thought, you ain't a girl.

She giggled.

She sat in a chair and licked the top of a cold Coors bottle. I sat on the coffee table. She had a thin and pointed tongue.

She shrugged her shoulders and grinned.

I said, "Where's your daughter?"

"Staying with friends."

I said, "Where's her dad?"

She frowned and looked at the television screen. No sound. Just the picture. Right then Montgomery Clift was beating the hell out of John Wayne.

"Where's her dad?"

"Santa Fe."

I sat down on the couch and she looked at me and leaned forward. The brown towel slipped just enough so I could see some cleavage.

She smiled. "I love this towel."

I wondered what she looked like without its protection.

I said, "He work for the state government or some-thing?"

She frowned. I noticed a lot of wrinkles on her forehead. "Is it important?"

I said, "Is it that bad?"

She grabbed the Coors and stuck the top between her lips and held the long neck with two fingers and a thumb as she took a sip. She nodded.

I said, "Can't be that bad."

She snorted and I wondered if the Coors got in her nose.

She shrugged again and got up and walked around and sat next to me on the couch. On the television some woman pointed a pistol at Montgomery Clift and John Wayne. I thought, that ain't right.

She snuggled next to me.

And said, "He's in the penitentiary."

I scooted away and looked at her.

Her mouth turned down and her face flushed and right then she was pretty ugly. I thought I saw a tear fall.

I said, "I'm sorry."

She nodded.

"What for?"

"Murder."

"Oh."

"Wasn't first degree. It was manslaughter. He beat a man to death in a fight. A Navajo. I don't think he meant to kill him." She looked at me and wrinkled her nose. The gleam from the overhead light reflected off her black eyes as she stared at me. She turned away, "But maybe he did."

"What do you mean?"

She said, "My husband's a Chicano. It happened in Gallup. In Gallup, the Chicanos hate Navajos."

I put my arm around her and pulled her closer. "I'm sorry."

"That's why I'm going to San Francisco."

"What do you mean?"

"He's getting out of the pen."

She laid her head on my shoulder. I kissed her on the neck. The smoothest neck I'd ever felt. I touched her calf just below the knee. The smoothest.

She giggled as she ran her fingers along the nap of the couch's fabric. Then stuck her tongue out and licked her bottom lip as she said. "I just love this towel." In the middle of the night she whispered, "I love your dick. I love your dick. I love your fucking dick."

Rifton T. slapped Tommy Carmona's palm and they clasped hands like the black dudes like to do and Carmona pulled Rifton T. right out of his chair. Carter beamed as he looked on.

Carmona hugged Rifton T. close and said, "We were a team, eh, R. T.?"

Rifton T. leaned back and said, "Yup."

"Remember that game against Springer, R. T.? You ran for over a hundred yards and I passed for over two hundred. We kicked their fucking asses."

"I recollect."

Carmona glanced at me. I hid my eyes on my red chili sauce. I took a bite. There must have been a chunk of real hot jalapeño in there. My mouth burned.

Carter butted in, "Hey, Tommy, whatever happened to that squaw you was married to?"

I felt Carmona's eyes on the top of my Stetson hat. Seared right through like sunbeams through a magnifying glass burning piss-ants in the dirt.

"Aw, she divorced me and ran off with our kid to hide in San Francisco."

"Sorry about that."

I looked up. Carmona glanced at me again and the color of his eyes surprised me. They were blue. Bright blue. Not like any Chicano I ever knew.

Carter took advantage, "How long you been out?"

Carmona flexed those fists. "Three weeks."

Her words came to me. "He beat a man to death."

The underarms of my shirt dripped sweat.

Rifton T. huffed, "You going to go fucking get her?"

Carmona didn't answer. He flexed his fists, again. He looked at me again. "Who's this?"

Rifton T. answered, "Excuse my poor manners. Tommy Carmona this is Al Sieber."

Carmona stuck out his right paw and I took it. He squeezed, but not hard. The soft palm surprised me. He squeezed harder and nodded at me.

Carter asked, "Well, are you going to go get her?"

Carmona shook his head and said, "She didn't love me, I guess. Didn't want to wait till I got out of that fucking pen."

Rifton T. nodded. "Probably off fucking some hippies or half-fags up there."

Carmona frowned and nodded as he looked at me.

"Guess she didn't love me."

Scabs

Sadie and I traipsed along gawking at the lights of tall buildings blinking through the drizzle. Taxis honked, tires emitting hisses as they spun on wet pavement. At a corner a gang of people jammed underneath the awning of a hotel yelling and banging on pot bottoms. They chanted little ditties and cursed, using the F-word a lot. I heard an amplified voice over the tops of the crowd. It was yelling, "Scab, f-ing scab." The voice had a rich timbre that reminded me of late nights when I was a kid. When the train whistle came out of the midnight hour, when I dug under my sheets and stretched my toes over the end of the bed.

I put my arm around Sadie and we walked towards the crowd. Mercedes and BMWs were lined up at the curb. T he crowd was rowdy and surged up to the doors of the cars and the hecklers hopped and screamed, "Scab, scab."

Sadie said, "Let's cross the street."

I said, "No. These people don't have any right to block the sidewalk."

She frowned. I hugged her close and smiled, whispered, "Don't worry, honey, we'll slip right on by."

I elbowed through the crowd, pulling Sadie along behind. The faces of the hell-raisers reminded me of faces I had seen in a book on Goya, noses bent out of shape, big knots above the eyes, chins that jutted.

The agitators made way for us, but frowned and glared. I could see the megaphone man. He was harassing a hotel employee helping a customer unload large leather bags from the back of a Jaguar. The megaphone was pointed right at the young man's face, and the words, "Scab, f-ing scab," hit him like sucker punches. I thought he might go down. He flinched at every word, squinted. The megaphone man grinned, hawk nose prominent, black eyes dancing, body tensed like he might do a lift-off. His cackle reminded me of sounds crows make when they harass from the tops of birch trees.

Our restaurant was down the street. I pulled on Sadie's arm, she pulled back, stared as the drama continued. I glanced at the employee, his eyes wide and darting, his shaking fingers, hunched shoulders. I looked at the megaphone man, watched his thick, angry lips as they formed the words, his perfect teeth as they chomped the C's and B's. I looked at his eyes, he noticed me.

He dropped the megaphone from his mouth. His eyes flared and then flashed as if he made fire from flint and steel. A spark in the steel wool. He smiled and started to say something. I grabbed Sadie's hand and jerked, pulled her away. She jerked back, said, "Hey, wait a minute."

I said, "We don't need to see that; besides, we've reservations."

She stood with her hands on her hips, drizzle clouding the scene behind the milling strikers, their anger. I yanked her arm again, she stumbled and followed. "OK," she said, "Don't rip my arm off."

As we hurried away I couldn't get those perfect teeth out of my mind, the flash of them in light, the smiles. And being in our teens hunting scorpions to turn in for a nickel apiece. Old rotted two-by-tens, sandy loam, wide-mouth mayonnaise jars with newspapers crumpled inside. The danger of it. The big scorpions, their dark yellow tint of old boards; the minute, clear-backed ones, deadly. The danger. And Mario, following behind. Trying to catch more than I.

And Saturday night sleepovers and the movies and after.

Him close, my toes stretched over the end of the bed and ...

Sadie said, "That was interesting. I've never seen anything like that."

I said, "Just your typical union BS."

She said, "Isn't it possible that they might be right?"

I said, "Nah," and sneaked a look behind, saw him standing there, the megaphone held dangling from his fingers.

And the hunting trip close to Mexico, sleet rattling our coat jackets like number six shot, our fathers gone after the old Jeep to carry the dead deer, the country rough, the ancient rusty rocks, scrappy edges that bit our feet. Us hiding under a juniper tree, as if someone would see us out there, and his thick lips and his tongue ...

Sadie said, "You're such an asshole sometimes. You know that?"

"How's that?"

"Everyone is supposed to agree with you."

I said, "Hey, those people are nothing but trouble."

And she said, "They are just people. Trying to get ahead. Like you and me. Not different, not ..."

I said, "And what do you feel for the 'scabs?'"

She said, "Them, too. I mean, just people, too."

And then later, when I was in the Corps, in sixty-eight, demonstrators outside the base gate, screaming anti-war slogans, we Marines with our unloaded guns, frightened, the rage, them throwing rotten eggs. And Mario, (and what the hell was he doing here ... in California in 1968, not in Arizona?) demonstrator *numero uno*, both hands loaded, ready to explode, and his surprised eyes locking mine and then rotten eggs flying and the stench, as bad as bodies left rotting in the sun; and his thick-lipped sneer, an invitation. And the secret meetings down in the Haight, me dressed in pink and purple see-through shirts, white bellbottoms, floppy Panamas, and the cramped small room, joints with stained ends and psychedelic light whirrs flashing on avocado-colored walls, his fat tongue, the silk sheets, my toes stretched over the end of the bed ...

Sadie was still lecturing as we got to the streetlight. "But don't you see? Sometimes people have to disrupt the normal flow of things. Just to make things right."

I said, "Every time these guys get a raise, it makes my cost of living go up. That's what I care about."

She scoffed and said, "You're greedy."

I asked her, "You think these people would give me money? You think they want to share with me?"

She said, "I think they would stand up for you if they thought you were being wronged."

I said, "Well you just go ask them. Ask them if they care about anybody but themselves."

She stopped and laughed. "Alright. Alright, I will."

As she turned away, I grabbed her arm and yanked her close, our faces almost touching. Her eyes full of disgust. Over her shoulder I could see him standing there. Like he wanted to call out.

I said, "I'm sorry. You're right, as always. We're going to be late and I'm hungry."

She smiled and pinched my cheek, "Oh, Jeff."

I pecked her lips and she moved close. I could feel her breasts against my chest. And the last time I saw him. When he showed without notice. Pissed me off. Me living in Martinez and all the coke lines he scratched on the coffee tabletop, and the shots of VO, and the party out on Grizzly Island; an old shack hidden on a back lane flanked by miles and miles of grain; thick heads loaded, droopy.

And strangers, and furious fists. And Mario, fresh off the picket lines in Salinas. Lettuce. Lettuce pickers. Mario strong. Defiant. He punched and flailed. And pistol shots. Mario down. Large blood stains on his stomach. His thick lips pulled back. His perfect teeth biting the night, the agony in his eyes. He reached his hand for me to help. His long fingers reminded me of Michelangelo sculptures. Someone kicked him in the side. He screamed. Someone called him

"Fucking asshole."

I kicked him in the side. I ran. The road home kept get-ting changed around in my mind. I ran out of gas near Lodi.

At the restaurant I looked back. I couldn't distinguish him from the rest of the milling, belligerent crowd. I held Sadie close. I could feel power pulse through her body. It infected me. Made the back of my head feel like someone had pumped it full of laughing gas. Happy.

About the Author

Photo by Kevin Martini-Fuller

Ken Rodgers lives and works in Boise, Idaho. He has been a sheepherder, a controller, a warrior, a real estate broker, a writer and a filmmaker, among other things. Ken has published three books of poetry: *Trench Dining*, *Barstow and Other Poems* and *Passenger Pigeons*. His short fiction and essays have appeared in a number of publications. Find out more about Ken's writing at kennethrodgers.com.

Ken served with the United States Marine Corps in Vietnam and survived the Siege of Khe Sanh in 1968. Along with his wife and co-producer, co-director, Betty, Ken made the feature length documentary film, *Bravo! Common Men, Uncommon Valor*, about that grim and terrible battle. You can find out more about the film at bravotheproject.com.